I Can See You

David Haynes

Copyright © David Haynes 2016. All Rights Reserved. No part of this document may be reproduced without written consent from the author

Edited by
Storywork Editing Services

Cover artwork by
Cover Collection

Formatting by
Polgarus Studio

To find out more about David Haynes and his books visit his Blog
http://davidhaynesfiction.weebly.com/
or follow him on twitter
@Davidhaynes71

The book quoted in Chapter 3 is from Clever Daddy by Maddie Stewart and Brita Granstrom and published by Walker Books

Maddie Stewart and Brita Granstrom

For Sarah and George.

Chapter 1

"Boom! Did you see that one, Dad?" Chris looked up and smiled but his dad just stared straight ahead. He looked like he was in that far-away place again.

"It was the biggest one yet," he added and turned away. In the cove below, the waves crashed onto the rocks and spat hissing white foam into the air. It was spectacular but Chris hadn't really wanted to come, not until he heard it was just going to be the two of them. Then he'd jumped at the chance to spend a few hours with his dad. *A boys' day out* was what they always called the days when it was just the two of them, but there hadn't been many recently. Not as many as there had been when he was five or six, anyway.

The headland in the distance seemed to be disappearing slowly. It was as if the clouds were gobbling it up.

"Is it a storm, Dad?" He tugged his sleeve. Dad couldn't ignore him that way.

"What?" He sounded like he'd just woken up.

"I asked if that was a storm?" Chris pointed out across the cove toward the black bags creeping across the horizon.

"It looks like it. We should head back to Granddad's now."

Chris's heart sank. How long had they been there? It didn't feel like it had been very long at all. He sidled into his dad's body and felt the warmth seep through the material of his jacket.

"Just a bit longer? I think the waves will get even higher." It was an obvious delaying tactic. He felt an arm go around his shoulder and the feeling in his stomach made him want to jump in the air.

"Just a few more minutes, Chris. Mum will be worrying."

Down in the cove, the waves smashed onto the slipway and raked at the stony beach. The sound they made was loud and frightening. Chris had never seen waves as high as this before, not even on the television, but that wasn't the real reason he wanted to stay. He was with his dad, just the two of them, and that was about as good as things got.

"What would happen if I fell in there?" He pointed at the waves.

The answer was instant. "I'd jump in and rescue you, of course."

"But what if a shark attacked you?" It was the sort of question he loved to ask his dad. It was a bit of a test as well as being fun.

He heard his dad laugh. It was little more than a sigh really but it was something. "Then I'd punch it in the eye and kick it in the goolies. See how he liked that."

They both laughed then and this time Chris felt his dad's chest heave. It was progress.

"It's not Scooby-Doo, Dad, and anyway I don't think sharks have goolies."

He laughed and felt a shuddering feeling through his arm. That was alright, Dad was really laughing now. He might be laughing so hard he was crying.

Crying?

Was Dad crying? Chris didn't dare look up in case he was. He didn't even want to think about it. He wished that thought had never come into his mind. He stamped his foot to try and push it away but it was too late, it was already there.

He'd heard Mum crying a few times. He'd heard Mum and Dad shouting at each other and she always cried afterwards. This was only at night, only when they thought he was asleep and couldn't hear them. But he did hear them and it always frightened him. He wouldn't tell them that though, because if he did then he might cry and that would just upset everyone. It wasn't all of the time, anyway. It just seemed that way at the moment.

A loud crack of thunder made him jump.

"I think we need to go now, the rain's on the way." Was there a tremble in his dad's voice?

Chris nodded. He didn't feel like staying here any longer anyway. He'd spoiled it for himself by thinking too much.

"Okay, Dad."

So that was the end of the *boys' day out*. What was waiting for him back at Granddad's? A few games of Top Trumps, perhaps? Or Granddad might tell him some stories about King Arthur and that was always exciting. He suspected Granddad made some of them up because he was sure there weren't any space rockets in the olden days, but the stories were always great. He'd even started making up a few of his own. They were no way near as good as Granddad's but they were okay. He might read them to Mum and Dad to cheer them up.

"Can we get fish and chips for tea?" He took his dad's hand as they walked back toward the car park. The first raindrops fell on his face and stung his cold cheeks.

"I'm not sure Mum's in the mood for fish and chips at the moment. Maybe tomorrow."

Chris nodded and felt his stomach flutter again as his dad squeezed his hand. He looked up at the car park. It was a good ten minute walk along the path, all uphill. He was probably too old for a piggyback now but there was no harm in trying his luck.

"My legs are tired."

"Are they now? I don't suppose a piggyback would help at all, would it?"

He shrugged and took an exaggerated step forward. "It might, Dad."

He felt hands take him under his armpits and hoist him skyward. He heard his dad grunt as he landed on his shoulders.

"You're heavy! I'll take you halfway and you can walk the rest. Okay?"

The wind buffeted them as they made their way along

the path and he could hardly hear what his dad was saying, but it barely mattered. This was as close as they'd been to each other for ages and to Chris it felt just about as good as anything he could ever remember. The smile on his face was so wide it almost hurt his cheeks.

They neared the end of the path, just before it took one final steep ascent to the car park, and he was lowered back down.

"Just give me a minute to catch my breath. That was a lot harder than I remember."

His dad was bent over and his face was bright red. His dark hair blew sideways across his face but Chris could see thin grey lines running through it now.

"You're getting old, Dad."

He looked up. There was false anger written across his face and it made Chris smile.

"Am I now?" He straightened. "I bet I could beat you up there." He pointed toward the car park.

"No chance. I'm the second fastest runner in my class." Chris could beat almost all of the other kids, except for Josh but he was the tallest in the class and had the longest legs.

They lined up side by side.

"Well, I'm the fourth fastest in all of my office. On the count of three. One, two…"

Chris set off. His legs pumped as fast as they could but the slope was steep and he could feel them slowing down almost immediately. He glanced over his shoulder but his dad hadn't caught up yet. He took three more steps and stopped.

"It's not fair, it's too steep for me." He looked over his shoulder but Dad was still on the start line. He hadn't moved an inch.

"Dad?" he called out but his words were driven away on the wind. "Dad?" he called again and started walking back down the slope. He wasn't even looking up at him. He was looking down into the cove.

"What is it?"

Without another word, his dad started running down the path toward the cove, toward the angry looking sea and… Was that a person standing on the slipway? It looked like it.

Chris set off immediately but he was already several steps behind his dad, who seemed to be running at top speed down the path.

"Dad! Wait for me!" Chris shouted, but he knew the wind and the sea had taken his words as soon as they came out of his mouth. His feet skidded on the dusty path, which wouldn't be dusty for much longer now the rain was coming down even heavier. The air smelled sharp and fresh like it did back up on the path but it was also much stronger down here. It smelled dangerous.

The path snaked down into the cove, passing the fishermen's huts on the way. Each one was pressed into the cliff face with a tumble of fishy-smelling lobster pots outside. He lost sight of his dad as he struggled to keep up and a moment of panic gripped him.

"Dad, Dad, Dad!" His throat felt sore from shouting and he knew he was close to crying. He skidded as the dirt path turned into concrete and as he fell painfully onto his bum, he let out a yelp. The tears came quickly but they were gone as soon as he saw his dad.

The air was filled with rain and salt water, and the noise was deafening. Dad was standing farther down the slipway and, a few steps on from him, there was a woman. The sea was up to her waist. Waves smashed into her chest, sending spray high into the air.

"Dad! Come back!" He was worried now. The water was white as far as he could see and Dad's feet were covered by it. It wasn't safe to be here.

But Dad hadn't heard him; he couldn't hear him and Chris was too afraid to go any closer. There was a steep drop on either side of the slipway, he knew that from the last visit, but the pebbles weren't visible anymore, it was just fizzing sea.

His dad waited for a wave to land on the woman and jumped forward to grab her. Her hair was wild and curly and it floated above her head like a brown cloud. A gust of wind sent both the woman and his dad wobbling sideways, and for a moment Chris thought they might fall over. Dad seemed to be trying to drag her out of the sea rather than helping her. Didn't she want to be rescued?

Dad looked angry and frightened at the same time but the woman just looked angry. Her mouth was open and she looked like she was shouting something at him. Chris couldn't hear any of it. Dad was covering his eyes and his ears now and he looked like he was in pain. Why was she hurting him when he was trying to help her?

"Dad?" He didn't want anyone to hurt him; not his dad.

His dad turned and looked at him and he felt as if everything had been turned upside down. Dad wasn't leading her out, she was leading him in.

"Leave him, leave my dad alone," he shouted but his voice wasn't loud enough. He started to cry again.

And then she turned to him. Where her eyes should have been, there were just holes, just deep black holes.

He didn't understand. It couldn't be real. But Dad was in the water and it was up to his waist and the waves were smashing into him.

"Help him!" he screamed.

She just stared back at him from where her eyes should have been.

Dad was screaming too, he was waving his arms. All Chris could hear was the word, "*Go!*" But how could he leave, how could he leave his dad when he needed help?

He ran toward him, toward her, but Dad shook his head. He didn't want Chris near him. He didn't want his help.

But she was there, she was looking at Dad again, and he was looking at her and crying. Dad was crying. Even above the sound of the wind and the rain, he could hear Dad crying.

He was going to be sick. He could feel it boiling in his guts. The waves were landing on Dad's head, pushing him down.

"Dad, no!" he screamed and ran forward.

But she was between them. She didn't want Dad to see him. As he looked up at her to tell her to move, she fixed him with those voids and spoke for the first time.

"I can see you."

He took two steps backwards. He needed to put some distance between them. Her voice cut through the wind as if she were inside his ears, inside his head. It was so clear and hideous. There was nothing inside those holes, nothing at all, and it made his head feel funny; like it did after a bad dream and he couldn't wake up properly. What did it mean to feel like that? It was sad and it was frightening. But it was terrifying above everything else.

"Stop! Chris!" He could hear Dad now. He was safe.

But his legs were moving and he couldn't stop them. He didn't want to.

"Chris!" Dad was coming. Dad would help him, he would help them both.

He vaguely felt that the earth had dropped away from his left foot. He was aware that she was still staring at him but he couldn't do anything about either. It was like her eyes were made of big round magnets. He was falling, he knew that, and when he'd finished falling he would be in the sea. It would be cold and he wasn't a good enough swimmer to cope with all those waves. He opened his mouth to scream but icy-cold water filled it immediately.

What had Dad said?

"I'd jump in and rescue you, of course."

But it looked like Dad needed rescuing too. They both needed rescuing.

Chapter 2

Chris stared up at the ceiling. He didn't need to check his phone to know what time it was. He'd woken up at the same time every day for the last week. It was probably more like a month but who was counting? Four-thirty on the dot. *She* had been with him most of the night too; standing right in the middle of his head, spreading her slimy fingers over everything. He couldn't remember the last night he had spent without *her* and those vapid pools of depression she called eyes.

Now came the choice. He could lie here, as still as a statue, and wait for the dawn to creep through the curtains. Then he could count the squares on the Anaglypta wallpaper, oh the joy. Or he could climb out of bed and go and watch the news downstairs. The second one was the better choice but it came with an added extra. It came with a question. It came with a well-meaning wife who wanted to help but didn't know how.

"Is everything alright, Chris?"

He could hear her breathing steadily, but it didn't seem to matter even if she was in the middle of a Brad Pitt fantasy-dream, she always snapped out of it as soon as he moved. He didn't want to hear the question again. He didn't want to hear it again because they both knew that the answer he gave was a lie.

"I'm fine, Lou, just go back to sleep."

No, this was the best idea. Just lie still until the alarm goes off in two hours time. He could do that. He *had* done it yesterday and the day before. It was easier than trying to answer a question he hadn't a clue how to reply to.

How cold had he become? How distant was he? Some days it felt as if he were bobbing about on the sea in a little boat and everybody else was on the shoreline; Lou, Ollie and everyone else he knew. And every day, they grew smaller and smaller until he could barely see their faces. He knew that one day he'd drift right over the horizon until they couldn't see him anymore. The way things were going, that wouldn't take long.

The only person who could say how cold he'd become was Lou. Ollie had never known anything different. To him, Dad had always been just Dad. Whether that was distant or not, he was just too young to know. But Lou, she knew. She never said anything, not yet at least, but the time would come when her patience was stretched too far, when the *"Is everything alright?"* questions were just words uttered out of habit rather than genuine enquiry.

He rolled over. The sad thing was, he knew what was

happening. He could feel it creeping through his bones, he could feel it in his gut. He could even feel it in his piss but how could he stop it? Now that was a question and the clock was ticking.

"Chris?"

He rolled onto his back again. Lou was awake. Had his thoughts woke her up? "It's early. Go back to sleep," he whispered.

"Okay?"

"I'm fine, just woke up early, that's all."

"Like yesterday?" She rolled onto her side to face him.

"Yeah, it's nothing. Go back to sleep."

"What time is it?"

He grabbed his phone. "Just after five." Had only half an hour gone by?

"I'm awake now too. Is it anything I can help you with?"

Light had started to filter into the room but it was going to be a grey day. In lots of ways.

"No, it's nothing, honestly. I'm just having a few problems with the book, that's all. It's nothing." How many times could he say the word *nothing* before it became *something?*

"I can help." She paused. "I can help, Chris."

"I know you can." She wasn't talking about the book. They both knew it. "Shall I put the news on?" he asked and grabbed the remote. In a minute the room would be filled by the voice of a newsreader, one of the unlucky ones from the night shift, but not by either his or Lou's voice and that was good. That was safe.

"I'll go and make us a cup of tea," he said and reached under the covers. Squeezing her hand was a gesture not only of affection but of placation. That was the end of the conversation. That was as far as it went.

She squeezed his hand back and they both smiled at each other.

"I love you," she whispered.

"I love you too, sweetheart."

He rolled out of bed and padded down the stairs.

And he did love her. God knew how much he loved her. He loved both of them so much that it ached to see how badly he was hurting them both. When he disappeared over that horizon and was lost completely, they might be better off. They might be able to forget him easier than the slow, almost ethereal vanishing act he was doing at the moment.

He stared out of the kitchen window and watched a couple of sparrows shuffle around the garden looking for their breakfast. Soon enough the ground would be too hard for their beaks to puncture. It didn't seem to be so long ago that Ollie had celebrated his birthday with a group of his friends in the garden. They'd all enjoyed the water-fight which had turned into a free-for-all despite Lou's best intentions.

He finished making the tea and grabbed a carton of orange smoothie out of the fridge. Ollie would be awake soon and the daily routine would start. Everyone knew what they had to do and in what order it needed to be done so that Lou was ready for work and Ollie was ready for school. That was how it was supposed to work, anyway. In reality it was a chaotic mess but at least it was a time of day that he wasn't left alone with his own thoughts. It was better that way.

He walked back up the stairs. By now Lou would be watching the news, and with any luck would be distracted enough to leave things as they were. He pushed the bedroom door open, doing his best not to slop any tea over the beige carpet. One look at Lou told him she wasn't watching the news. How could she be when her eyes were full of tears?

If he asked her what was wrong, which he should do, then he knew where it was going. He didn't need to, though, because Lou spoke first.

"I know what's happening here, Chris. I know."

He put the tea down and sat on the edge of the bed with his back to her.

"I know what this year means and…"

"We don't need to talk about this."

"Yes, yes we do for both mine and Ollie's sake, we have to talk about it."

He rubbed the back of his neck. He could feel the tension sneaking up on his muscles. A headache would follow very soon but that was okay. It was another excuse for not writing anything worth a jot.

"I don't know what to say, Lou. I don't know where to begin."

"The start?"

He felt her arms circle around him and her lips on his naked shoulder. Lou knew everything about what had happened. When he'd shared it with her, a long time ago, it had felt good to be able to say the things which had gone around and around in his head for so long. It had been a relief to finally say the words.

"I killed my dad." There, that was the start. "Is that what you wanted to hear again?"

He turned to face her. "I killed him, Lou. I… killed… him." It never felt right to utter those words and it never would, no matter how many times he said it. "How was that for you? Want me to tell Ollie too?"

In the dim morning light, he could see the pools which gathered at the corners of her eyes. They overflowed and ran down her cheeks, and it ripped a hole in his guts. He regretted his words instantly.

"I'm sorry." But it was too late. She shrank away from him and flopped back on the bed.

"I can't go on like this," she said. "Neither of us can."

They both sat there in silence for a minute.

"Mum!" Ollie's voice cut through the atmosphere for which Chris was relieved.

"I'll go," he said and stood up.

"No, he wants me." Lou slid off the bed beside him and slipped the dressing gown over her naked body.

Chris held out the smoothie. "I'm sorry," he whispered but Lou was already out of the door on her way to their son.

A few minutes passed and he could hear muffled voices coming from Ollie's room. He'd been wetting the bed recently and was getting anxious about it, overly anxious in Chris's opinion. He'd wet the bed too; nearly every night for a year after…

"Chris?" Lou's voice came through loud and clear. The newsreader was talking about dying immigrants off the coast of Italy. He'd been watching the pictures but the words were a meaningless babble.

"Coming." He walked into Ollie's room expecting to see his upset and wet son clinging to Lou. Instead, Ollie was beaming up at him, holding a sheet of paper close to his chest.

"What's this?" Chris smiled back at him.

"I've drawn you a picture, Dad. I drew it last night but it wasn't quite finished. Now it is." He pushed the sheet toward Chris who took it.

Ollie could make his heart melt just by breathing but when he looked like this, Chris just wanted to hold the image of his son in his head for as long as he could.

"Look at it then!" Ollie was impatient for his dad to look at the masterpiece. He shuffled forward toward the edge of the bed.

Chris turned the picture around and stared. He couldn't speak.

"Can you see, Dad?" Ollie was tapping the top of the paper with his finger. "There's you, me and Mum on the beach in France." Their likenesses were all clearly labelled and all the colours were truly vivid. They were the colours of the world in a child's mind. But it wasn't the drawings of Lou or Ollie or himself that made his heart sound like a bass drum in his ears. There was someone else in the picture.

"And that's Granddad." Ollie sounded and looked really pleased with himself. "Can you see him? Look, he's there."

Ollie grabbed the picture and tapped the spot.

There was a picture of a black stick-man lying on top of the intensely blue sea. He was some way in the distance but beneath him Ollie had written the word 'GRANDDAD'S DEAD.' There was an ugly red smudge where Granddad's head should have been and his eyes were crosses.

Chris looked at Lou, whose own eyes showed nothing, and then back at the picture again.

"Only we can't see him because we're looking the wrong way." Ollie sounded disappointed now as if his artistic skills had let him down.

The room was silent for a moment before Chris handed the picture back to Ollie. He smiled at his son but it felt forced and thin. He opened his mouth to speak but he realised he didn't have a clue what to say, and left the room.

"Didn't he like it?" He heard Ollie's question to Lou.

He didn't hear her reply because he was already halfway down the stairs, heading toward his office. He needed a few minutes to collect his thoughts. He pushed the door open and stepped inside. This was his place of work. This was the place where he'd written the four novels which had enabled him to pack in the job at the hospital and go full time. This was the place where he'd sat day after day for most of the last year and stared into space.

He slumped onto the swivel chair and turned it to face the window. The view was as familiar as the lines on the back of his hand, or the tea-stain on the letter A on his keyboard. They were all things he knew well.

Ollie didn't know much about his granddad. He didn't

know about the accident, where it was or any of the details. Maybe when he got older he might ask but for now, he didn't need to know anything other than the fact that Granddad wasn't around now. Besides, Lollipop Joe, his great-granddad, was enough old man for anyone. Was it just a coincidence that Ollie had drawn him floating on the sea like that? Or had the information come from somewhere else? Lou, maybe. Why would she do that?

There was a bang on the door and then Lou came in.

"Ollie thinks he's upset you. Can you go and put your arms around him please?"

Chris swivelled around. "Did you tell him about Dad?"

She shook her head. "Of course not. If and when he asks about Jack that'll be your job, not mine."

He stared at her for a moment and rubbed at the stubble on his face. "Why did he draw him like that? Floating about on his back with blood coming out of his head. He shouldn't have done that."

"What? What are you talking about?"

Chris stood up. He could feel anger and frustration starting to bubble. Neither seemed very far from the surface at the moment.

"The picture, Lou. The *fucking* picture of my dad that our little boy just drew. I'm pretty sure you can remember it."

"Don't swear, Chris. I'm not sure what you saw on that page but it wasn't *that*." She paused and licked her lips. "Chris, you need to come and see your boy and you need to do it now."

Chris looked away again, out of the window where there was nothing but the hulking silhouettes of the oak trees in the field across the road.

"Well?" Lou sounded angry.

There was a pause and then he heard the door close again. He wanted to go straight upstairs and pick Ollie up. He wanted to kiss his forehead and tell him Daddy was struggling a bit at the moment so he just needed to be patient with him. There was that picture, though. Why had Ollie drawn it like that? He jumped up and kicked the chair. It toppled into his desk and came to rest on two legs. It looked exactly how he'd been taught to leave his chair at the end of a school day. School hadn't worked out too well either.

He walked into Ollie's room. The curtains were open and Ollie was trying to read his Lego comic. He looked up and Chris could immediately see the worry in his eyes.

"I'm sorry, Dad. I didn't mean to…"

Chris took Ollie in his arms and hugged him. "Shh. You've done nothing wrong. The picture was perfect, I was just thinking about something else, that's all." Ollie wasn't ordinarily a big hugger but Chris could feel the strength of the boy's arms around him. Neither of them were in any hurry to let go.

"Dad?" Ollie finally eased himself away.

"Yes?"

"You know at your party on Sunday, can I ask Jake to come? Mum said it'd be okay but she said to check with you first. I think I might be bored otherwise."

The party. The party to celebrate turning *The Big Four-*

Oh. Lou had organised it, at first secretly, and then less so when emails and texts had started coming in. He didn't want it. In fact it was the last thing he wanted. It was the same age his dad had been when…

"Dad?" Ollie's voice shook him out of his thoughts.

"Sorry, what was that?"

"I asked you about Jake?"

"Of course it is, that's fine." He broke free of his son's grip and kissed his head. The boy immediately wiped it off.

"Ten more minutes and then it's time to come and have breakfast."

He started to walk out and then turned around.

"Why did you draw Granddad like that?"

Ollie shrugged. "I asked Lollipop about him last summer and he told me Granddad was out in the ocean somewhere and he was swimming around the world. He said Granddad just kept swimming and swimming and swimming and one day we'd all see him again."

Chris nodded. It was just like Lollipop to make up something on his feet like that. The man had a sharp and creative mind.

"But why the blood? Is Granddad hurt?"

"Blood? I didn't draw any blood, Dad."

Chris stepped toward Ollie. "Where's the picture?"

Ollie rummaged under his duvet and dragged it out. "I was going to throw it away because you didn't like it."

Chris took the picture and examined it. The vivid colours were the same, as were the three of them, but something had changed. His dad, Ollie's granddad, was no longer the lifeless corpse with a red smudge for a head. He looked like he was bobbing around in the sea and drawn across his face was an enormous smile. He held one hand up like he was waving and beneath him was the word GRANDDAD. Nothing more.

"Have you changed it, Ollie? Is this the same picture?"

"No, it's the same one I showed you."

He looked at Ollie for a sign that the boy was being mischievous. This wasn't the right time for that.

"You must have. Granddad was just floating a few minutes ago and his head…" He took the picture over to the window where the light was better and tried to look for a sign that the red smudge had been erased. There was nothing.

He walked back to the bed. "Ollie, what have you done to the picture?"

Ollie looked worried. "I haven't done anything, Dad. Honestly."

Chris looked at the picture and then back at Ollie again. He could feel a knot in his stomach and it was twisting painfully.

Lou came into the room. "What's this?"

"Did you ask him to change it?" he asked her.

"Change what?"

This was turning into something it didn't need to be but he couldn't stop it. "This." He waved the picture in front of her.

Lou took it from him and looked at it. "Chris, what are you talking about? It's the same picture he showed you earlier."

He snatched it off her and waved it in the air. "He drew my dad with his head bashed in and he'd written 'granddad's dead' under it. I'm not stupid, I know what I saw."

He could hear Ollie snivelling in the background and Lou walked over to him.

"Chris, just stop it, you're frightening him. Just give it a rest."

He looked at the pair of them and then at the picture. It was just a simple picture drawn by a boy, that was all. There was nothing spiteful or evil about it. It was just a picture.

"I'm sorry, I'm not sure…" He ended there. There was no point in continuing. Neither of them would want to hear anything else that came from his mouth.

"I'll just…"

Lou waved him away. Ollie's face was buried in her chest. He wandered downstairs, into his office and shut the door. Another successful start to the day.

He powered up the laptop and waited for it to run its usual start-up routine. It was habit more than necessity these days. He couldn't remember writing anything half-decent for about a year now. It was a good job his backlist was still selling well because without that, things would be more than a little grim.

He wasn't mistaken about Ollie's drawing though. He knew what he'd seen.

Chapter 3

Lou had arranged every detail for the party and that meant it would be perfect. Chris supposed she thought it might distract him but it was the exact opposite. All it had done was put a huge red ring around the date and made him think about it even more. It made him think about the significance of his age.

She had invited everyone he knew, some people he didn't know and some he wished he had never met. He walked into the garden with the look of a man who was absolutely shocked by all the people there; someone who was delighted at the effort gone into organising a surprise party for him. The look was forced and false but he hoped that was unreadable.

He stepped into the crowd as they clapped him on the back and shook his hand. He wished he was somewhere else. Anywhere else would do.

"How's my big boy?" Chris smelled his mum's perfume before he felt her lips on his cheek.

His dad hadn't had a huge fortieth celebration, but then again his relationship with his wife had been even worse than his and Lou's. Or maybe she'd listened to her husband and not organised one.

"Hi, Mum." She didn't look her age but she never had. "Ken." He took his mum's partner's outstretched hand and shook it. "Thanks for coming."

"You don't look thrilled, Chris." His mum took his hand after Ken had released it and held it.

He was trying hard to maintain the facade of the happy birthday boy and didn't think it had slipped already.

"Does it show?"

She leaned a little closer. "No, but I know you and I know what's going on in there." She let go of his hand to touch his temple. "I don't need to be mind reader for that."

Chris smiled and kissed her cheek. "Have you got a drink?"

Ken held his flute up. "Lou's been round already."

"That's good. I'll see you in a bit. I suppose I've got to circulate." He started to walk away but his mum grabbed his wrist.

"Dad would be proud of you."

Chris felt his stomach turn but he managed a smile before she let go. He walked through the crowd to the table where the drinks were. He grabbed the largest glass he could find and poured himself a very large white wine. He downed it in one and poured himself a second.

"Better go steady there, sweetheart." Lou was by his side.

"I just need something to get me through this." He took

a drink, draining half of the glass.

"Is it that bad? It wasn't supposed to be such an ordeal, Chris."

He looked at her. She looked tired and although she was trying to smile, she was sad. He could see it in her eyes. It was crippling.

"It's perfect, Lou." He tried to look earnest.

"Don't lie." She touched the glass. "Just don't ruin it, that's all I ask."

He swallowed the remainder of the wine and poured another. "I won't and that's the last one, I promise."

"Okay, well Ollie wants to toast you so…"

He held up his hand. The first glass of wine had started buzzing through his brain already and it felt good. "I'll be on my best behaviour. Now go and circulate."

She smiled and kissed him. "I love you."

"I love you too," he replied.

The party must have cost a fortune. There were waitresses weaving through the crowd with trays of food and glasses of wine, and there were even a pair of cellists huddled under a parasol. It was more likely to be used as an umbrella rather than a shield for the non-existent sun. There had to be more than fifty people here.

"Boo!"

He jumped a little and spilled wine down his shirt.

"Good party, Dad?" He hadn't seen or heard Ollie approaching but he was standing right beside him with a huge smile on his face. His best friend Jake was with him.

"The best. You two enjoying it?" He put his hand on

Ollie's shoulder.

Ollie shrugged. "It's okay. Is Lollipop Joe coming?"

Joe was his great-granddad but acted like a granddad, and according to Ollie was the coolest man on earth.

"I don't think he could make it but we'll see him again soon." There weren't many people he could stand to be at this party with, but Joe was one of the select few.

"Okay."

There was a moment of silence between them before Jake pushed a card forward. "This is from my family. Happy birthday."

Ollie snatched it away instantly. "It's not his birthday until tomorrow and I'm in charge of putting the cards and presents in the kitchen. You can help me if you like."

The two boys ran off without another word. Chris watched them.

He hadn't asked Lou about Joe but he didn't need to. Joe wouldn't want to be at something like this any more than he did. He didn't blame him. There would probably be a phone call from him tomorrow to wish Chris a happy birthday. Joe had been more like a dad than a granddad afterwards and he loved him like one. He looked over at his mum. She'd kept him away from Joe's for a long time afterwards and that had created some bad feeling between them.

"Chris, come and tell us about your next book." He recognised some relatives he hadn't seen for about two years. He smiled and topped up his glass. They would be easy to talk to. There wouldn't be any difficult questions about… well, about his dad.

"Everyone, can I have your attention please!" Lou's voice carried above the hum of conversation. "There's someone here who wants to say a few words."

Ollie was standing on a stool and in his hands he clutched a sheet of paper. He put his hand to his mouth and coughed theatrically. He'd always been just the right side of confident but he looked a little nervous.

Everyone had a glass of champagne in their hands but Chris had two. Surely as the guest of honour he was allowed that? His head was spinning more than it should but he'd held it together for the past three hours and hadn't sloped off to sit in his office, as much as he wanted to. That in itself was a triumph.

"I wanted to say a few words about my dad." Ollie sounded grown-up as he read from his script. Had he written it himself, Chris wondered?

"My daddy's very clever. He's a very clever man. He does all sorts of things like clever daddies can. He can swirl me, he can twirl me. He can swing me round and round. He can hold me high and fly me. He can swoosh me to the ground…"

Chris recognised the words immediately. They were from a book he'd read to Ollie when he was little more than a baby. The first time Ollie had said the word *shoe* was when the illustration showed the little boy's shoes flying off as the daddy swung him around and around.

Ollie carried on reading and Chris could feel a mist drop

over his eyes. His vision was becoming blurred, not from the wine but from the tears that were pooling in his eyes. Lou had bought him the book when Ollie turned one. Although he hadn't heard the words for years, he remembered them perfectly and mouthed them in time with Ollie.

"He hugs me and he cuddles me and tucks me up with Ted. Night night, Daddy. Night night, sleepy head! Happy birthday, Dad!"

It was no use, he couldn't hold the tears back any longer. A great stream ran down his cheeks and fell onto his shirt. Everyone was clapping and through blurred vision, Chris started walking toward his son.

And then he stopped dead in his tracks.

"You?" He wiped the tears away from his eyes and blinked. "Why are you here?"

Right behind Ollie, he could see her standing with her hands on his shoulders. Her hair was a tangle of seaweed and her skin was white, too white. He thought he was about to vomit. He'd seen her every night for the last year but only in his dreams.

"Get away from him!" he screamed.

He was aware of the hush and of the expressions of the people either side of him. It seemed like they had parted to make way for him.

"Chris, stop it!" He heard Lou's voice come from somewhere out in front but his vision had narrowed and all he could see was his son and *her*, one in front of the other. She looked hellish and water rolled down her face in a continual sheet. It hid her expression but he knew what was beneath the water. He'd looked into those eyes before, he'd looked into those holes and it had nearly killed him.

He started walking again. It wasn't possible, of course it wasn't, and yet she was there. She was there.

"Dad?" Ollie sounded frightened. It was the voice he used in the middle of the night when a nightmare woke him. It was the voice of a scared little boy. It sounded like his own voice had when the lady had looked at him. The lady whom nobody had ever found.

"Please, Dad."

"It's okay, Ollie. I'm coming to save you!" He sprinted toward his son.

There was a collective gasp from the crowd and then Lou screamed at him. "Chris, stop it. Just stop it!" She grabbed his arm and he turned.

"But *she's* there. Look!" Chris turned and raised his finger. Ollie was frozen to the spot and his eyes were wide in shock.

But there was nobody behind him now. Ollie was on his own and tears were rolling down his cheeks. Chris stepped toward him but Lou pushed him to the side.

"Don't," she snarled.

"She was there. She was there," he muttered weakly.

And then all at once he was aware of everyone looking at him, staring at him. In their minds, they were thinking he was crazy; a bona fide lunatic of the highest order. He turned a full circle and stared back. Some of them actually had their mouths open. Under his stare, they turned away and started walking toward the house.

"I saw her!" Chris shouted. "I saw her." But his was the only voice now and he collapsed to his knees on the grass. He had managed to destroy the party in the most spectacular of fashions and had scared the hell out of Ollie in the process. Then there was Lou and her last words to him. *"Just don't ruin it, that's all I ask."*

Oh, but he had ruined it. He had ruined the shit out of it. He watched Lou put her arms around their weeping son and lead him away with everyone else. He was alone where only five minutes ago there had been a throng of people chatting away in the early autumn sun.

He allowed his body to topple forward and fall face-first into the turf.

"I saw her," he said to the grass.

*

"You need to go, Chris."

He watched Lou bundle his clothes into the suitcase. Tears had caused her make-up to run and black streaks ran down her cheeks in smudged zigzags.

"You need to get your head straight."

There was no use in fighting it. She was right. He needed to go so he couldn't hurt them anymore.

"Is this for good?" he asked.

She looked up at him. "Just get your head straight, Chris."

He nodded and took a step toward her. "What about Ollie? Can I see him?"

Lou straightened. "You frightened him this afternoon

and it isn't the first time you've done that, is it? Do you know how proud he was to read that story? He'd been practising it every night for the last two months. He didn't need the paper to read it from, he knew every letter off by heart."

"I loved it. I was crying." He felt ashamed, utterly ashamed.

"And you ruined it. You ruined everything."

"But I saw…"

Lou held up her hand. "I don't want to hear it." She closed the case and held it up for him.

He took it from her. The hangover had started almost as soon as his head hit the turf and his tongue didn't feel the right size for his mouth.

"I'll go, Lou, but I want to see him before I do. I'm not leaving him like this."

She nodded. "He asked for you a while ago."

Chris lowered the case and walked into Ollie's room. He had no idea what he was going to say but an apology was a good place to start.

Ollie had his Batman torch on and was doing his best to read a comic. Chris could see his lips moving as he spelled out the words.

"Hey, big man."

Ollie snapped his head round and grinned. "Dad!" He stretched his arms out for a hug.

Chris felt tears try to come but he clenched his jaw together as hard as he could and they stayed away. He pulled Ollie toward him.

"Careful, Dad, you nearly dragged me out of bed."

He could tell by Ollie's voice that the boy was still smiling. That was good. He pulled back and kissed him on the forehead.

"I'm sorry I messed up earlier. I loved what you said. It was… it was…" He realised he didn't have the words. Nobody would.

"It was awesome!" Ollie laughed.

"Yep, that about covers it."

Ollie wriggled back under the duvet and picked up the comic again. It made Chris want to cry.

"Listen, I've got to go away to work on my book for a while."

He didn't look up. "Are you going to Lollipop's?"

He hadn't thought about where he might go but Ollie's suggestion was a pretty good one. "Yes, I might just do that."

"How long for?"

That was the million dollar question. "I'm not sure at the moment but I'll phone you every day and maybe when I'm… when I've nearly finished the book, you and Mum can come down and stay for a few days. How's that sound?"

Ollie looked up but his eyes weren't full of the excitement a trip to Lollipop's usually instilled. "You scared me, Dad. I didn't like it."

Chris swallowed hard. "I know and I'm sorry, Ollie, I'm so sorry. I just drank too much wine. Stay away from that stuff, it makes you behave very badly."

Ollie nodded and went back to his comic. The damage was already done, though, and Ollie would probably remember this day for the rest of his life.

He leaned over and kissed him again. "Right, I've got to go now. I'll call you tomorrow. Okay?"

Ollie jumped up. "If you're not going to be here tomorrow then you've got to open this!" He reached under the jumble of old teddy bears at the foot of the bed and dragged out a square about the same size as a netbook. It was wrapped in brightly coloured paper.

"I wrapped it too," he said proudly. "Mum! Dad's opening his present, come and watch!"

He heard Lou behind him but he didn't look at her. He didn't trust himself to look at either of them without turning into a blubbering idiot and that would complete the day perfectly.

He picked at the tape on either end of the parcel and slid the present out. It was a simple black frame and inside was a black and white photograph.

"Grandma let us have it and Mum sent it to a special shop where they made it bigger." Ollie was touching the frame. "That's you, isn't it Dad? And that's Granddad next to you. He looks loads like you."

Chris stared at the picture. Or more correctly, he stared at his dad's face. This was how he remembered the man, not the ghostly apparition he saw in his dreams or in Ollie's drawings. This was his dad. It had obviously been taken on a family holiday, not that he could remember which one. Both of them were smiling and in the background was the familiar outline of the Cornish coast, just down the lane from Lollipop's house. Chris had his arms folded and his dad was making bunny ears behind his head. It looked like they were both wearing rain jackets.

"I want to do that to you, Dad."

Chris could feel a smile breaking on his face. He wouldn't have been much younger than Ollie was right now. In fact, the picture was probably taken a year before… His smile retreated back into the shadows.

"Do you like it?"

Chris grabbed Ollie and held him. "It's perfect." His voice trembled.

Chapter 4

The radio said one lane of the motorway was closed after junction 28 but it barely mattered at this time of the night. He didn't have the radio on for the traffic news, only to keep him awake. It had been about five hours since his last drink, and his brain felt tight and dehydrated. He reached over for the water he'd bought at the petrol station and drained the last few drops.

As soon as Ollie had mentioned Lollipop, Chris knew it was the right place to go to try and sort his head out. Joe didn't ask a lot of questions, not out loud anyway. There had only ever been an arm around the shoulder and a few words of comfort from him. They had a lot in common, not all of it particularly good.

Sometimes Chris had to force himself to remember that not only had *he* lost his dad but Joe had lost a son. This is what had brought them closer together and kept them tight. There was nobody else who had lost quite as much when

Jack Kestle had died in the Atlantic Ocean. His mum had lost a husband and someone she had once loved but their relationship, had it endured past that day, would have ended in divorce sooner rather than later. That unspoken fact kept her out of the 'Joe and Chris club' and it set her apart from them both.

He had no idea what he was going to do when he got there or how being there would help him, but that's where both his heart and head told him to go. He glanced at the passenger seat and saw the framed picture Ollie had given him. Leaving him was the hardest thing he'd ever done in his life but it was necessary. Lou knew it and so did he.

The melancholy that had dominated his mind for the last year was now manifesting itself in hallucinations. That couldn't be good news. There had been a lack of clarity to his thoughts, a lack of energy and creativity. He knew this was down to how he was feeling but the apparitions were something different entirely. They were invasive and destructive in the worst way possible.

He allowed the car to drift across the lanes and exited the motorway. He didn't need a sat-nav to direct him, he'd made this journey hundreds of times. First in the back of the car and later as the driver. The route was as familiar to him as the short walk to Ollie's school.

He hadn't contacted Joe to tell him he was on his way, or that he had a suitcase full of clothes in the boot. That was a conversation to be had in person, not on the telephone in the middle of the night. Besides, Joe would open the door to him whatever the time, whatever the reason. He pushed the car up to seventy and switched on the cruise control. This stretch of road was straight, and at nearly two in the morning he wasn't likely to be making any sudden manoeuvres.

Ollie loved it down here. They all did, Lou included, and they came as often as they could. The best times were before Ollie had started school and they could come down in the early autumn when it was quiet. If they were lucky, they might have an Indian summer and spend days on the beach eating picnics and paddling in the sea, but if the weather wasn't so good then it didn't really matter. Ollie would still dig about in the sand and build sandcastles. He'd just be wrapped up in hundreds of layers of clothes to keep the wind out. They all would.

The first time Ollie's little toes had touched the sea, he squealed and thrashed his legs about like an Olympic sprinter. The second time he'd giggled and shouted, "Cold!" and then kicked at the ripples left by the dying waves. Chris had stood with the bottom of his jeans rolled up, holding onto his little boy as tight as he could. "Too tight, Daddy!" Ollie had said but he wasn't loosening his hold, not for anybody. No matter that the water barely covered his own feet.

Not once had they gone down to Hawk's Cove though. Chris had never been back since that day. He wasn't sure he would ever have the strength to go there again. He certainly couldn't take Ollie down there.

Just seeing the signpost in the village was hard enough. The dirty white letters on the faded green background reminded him that Hawk's Cove had been there longer than any of them and would be there as long as the ocean permitted it to remain. It was permanence where other things were not.

On the first occasion he'd come with Lou, he simply pointed at the sign without looking at it and said, "There." They hadn't been talking about it at the time but she didn't ask what he was referring to. There was no reason to, she just knew.

He checked the time. With one last stop for fuel, it would be another hour and a half before he reached Joe's cottage. That would make it after three. He felt guilty about waking him. Joe was in superb shape but waking a ninety-one year old man at that time of the night was bad form. He eased down on the pedal to disengage the cruise control and pushed the car up to eighty-five. He doubted there would be many traffic officers about on this stretch of road. If he could shave twenty minutes off the time, he would be up to talk to Ollie before he went to school.

He bit his lip to stop the tears coming and pushed down on the pedal a little harder.

*

Joe's place was the last in a row of fishermen's cottages. As Chris pulled onto the unadopted lane, his headlights picked out the partially submerged rocks which formed the road. Usually he might have tried to pick his way through the worst of them but tonight he just wanted to get into bed. He turned around the side of the house and immediately saw that the kitchen light was on. It was a bit late for the old boy to be up.

He cut the engine and stretched his back against the seat. He wouldn't bother getting the suitcase out of the boot tonight, it would just provoke questions. He opened the door and was about to climb out when he saw a figure standing at the back door.

He stepped out. "Granddad?" The kitchen light lit his face from the side but it was obvious he was smiling.

"Come in, son. Lou phoned and told me you were on your way."

Chris walked over and flung his arms around him. Despite his best efforts, he started to blubber almost immediately, and the sensation of Joe's hand patting him on the back only made it worse.

"Let's get inside before you wake the neighbours, eh?"

Chris took a deep breath and stepped inside. "Christ, I'm sorry about that, Granddad, I don't know where it came from."

Joe walked straight over to the microwave and started it up. "I think we'll make this one Irish." He reached up and opened a cupboard. In amongst the tins of food, Chris could see a jar full of brightly coloured lollipops and a half-finished bottle of Bushmills. Joe pulled the bottle out and put it beside two mugs he had ready and waiting.

"Do you want to talk?"

Chris shook his head. "No."

"Good because neither do I. I've made up your bed and you can take this up when it's ready. It'll help us both get off to sleep."

"I hope so," he replied.

The microwave beeped and Joe lifted the hot milk out. He poured it into the two mugs, added a little sugar and topped it up with whiskey. Steam rose up and the spicy smell drifted over to him.

"I've made it a large one. You look like you need it." Joe handed him the cup.

He looked down at the milk. It had turned a beautiful pale caramel colour. If anything was going to help him sleep, it was this.

"Right, I'll see you in the morning. You know where everything is."

Chris felt Joe's hand on the top of his head but as he raised his eyes, Joe had already gone. He waited a minute until the creaking floorboards above his head had stopped and then followed Joe up.

The room was the only double in the house but Joe had moved into one of the other singles years ago. He always maintained there was no point in having a double all to himself, not when he had no intention of ever sharing his bed again. Chris stripped off and climbed into bed. This was the room he always stayed in with Lou. The third bedroom, little more than a box, was where Ollie slept. Although usually by the time morning came, Ollie was either in their room or taking up most of Lollipop's bed.

He sipped the milk and tasted the toasted spice of the whiskey as it slipped down his throat. He hadn't had a drink of whiskey since the last time they'd been here, which was what? Just over a year ago. He activated his phone and set an alarm for seven. It was just over four hours away but he would be awake to talk to Ollie, no matter what.

He finished the drink and put the mug on the boards beside the bed. The wind hummed gently around the eaves and he felt himself drift away. Somewhere, not too far away, the waves thrashed the rocks in Hawk's Cove and hissed with spite. The sound crept up the lane toward Joe's cottage and wriggled in through a slender crack in the wall. It slithered through the house until it found someone it had tasted before.

*

How long had it been since he'd been here? Thirty-three years, that was how long, and yet nothing had changed. The rock formations, the outline of the coast and the waves all looked exactly the same. He took a deep breath. Even the clean metallic smell of the ocean was the same. There was familiarity but there was no sense of pleasure. This was the spot where he watched the waves on the day he killed his dad.

The sky was a deep grey that could only mean rain was on its way, and the strength of the wind meant it would be with him sooner rather than later. There were no fishing boats out on the ocean today. They knew better than to risk being out in the storm that was heading this way.

He'd have to go back to the car park soon if he didn't want to risk a drenching. And yet he wanted to leave it as long as possible. The longer he waited, the more chance he'd have of seeing… who?

Down in the cove, the slipway was partially submerged

in the turning tide. Soon it would be entirely covered and then…

Who was that down there? There was someone standing up to their knees in the water. It wasn't safe to be there when there was a storm coming. It wasn't safe. He ought to go and tell them, to pull them to safety, just like his dad had done.

And yet if he went down there…

He opened his mouth and shouted as loud as he could but his words were blown in the opposite direction by the wind. He could almost see the letters scattered in an incomprehensible jumble along the coast behind him.

The waves crashed into the figure's legs and made them stumble backwards. It was no good, he had to go down there. He ran back along the path, swearing under his breath. Whoever it was probably thought they were being daring, or brave or something else, but in reality they were just being stupid.

He called out again as he reached the first of the huts. The smell of the lobster pots was strong and unpleasantly bitter. He noticed as he passed them that each of the pots was crammed full of the rotting corpses of crabs, lobsters and fish. The stench was hideous.

He fell as he reached the slipway. Hadn't he done that once before?

"Hey you! It isn't safe. You need to come back up."

To his own ears, his voice was sharp and loud, impossible to ignore, and yet the figure didn't move an inch, just stared out at the storm.

He took a dozen steps and shouted again. "I said it isn't

safe. You need to..."

It was a man. He could see that now by his build and hair. His chestnut hair, with more than just a few grey streaks flashing through it, flew out at the sides like wings. Just like his own.

"Dad?" he whispered.

He jogged down the slipway. The sound of his heart beating was louder than the sound of the waves trying to smash the cove to bits.

"Dad!" He yelled this time and as he reached him, he put his hand out and touched his shoulder. It was wet and not just wet from standing in the rain or from being splashed by the sea but deep, deep down wet. Like his bones were filled with salt water, icy-cold salt water. It didn't feel right. It didn't feel right at all and he took his hand away immediately. He stared at his fingers and watched as raindrops jumped about on his flesh. Only the drops of water weren't clear like they should be; they were rust coloured, like they were contaminated with something. But the rust was darkening, and now it wasn't rust anymore, it was thick congealed blood, running down his hands and covering his arms.

He looked up. "What's happening to me?"

And as his dad turned around to face him, Chris screamed like the little boy he now was.

Where the warmest of eyes had once been were now pools of the most fathomless water imaginable.

A blackened, leathery eyelid dropped down and then flashed up again in a revolting wink. "I can see you," he said through a twisted, ugly snarl.

*

Chris almost jumped out of bed. He was sure he'd been screaming.

"Steady on there, boy."

He jumped again at the sound of Joe's voice. Joe was standing next to the bed with a mug of tea in his hand.

He rubbed his eyes. "What time is it?"

"Nearly half past six. I had a lie-in this morning."

Chris blinked and stretched his facial muscles. His head felt woolly and the remnants of the nightmare were slow to clear. He took the tea. "Was I shouting?"

"I've heard worse," Joe said.

After that day, Chris had wet the bed and screamed in his sleep for nearly a year. A lot of those times he'd been here in this very house; in the room reserved for Ollie's visits. That was before his mum decided it was a bad place for him to be and took him away.

"Sorry."

"I'm going out for my walk and when I get back we'll have eggs."

Chris nodded and took a drink of the tea. He never took it with sugar unless he was here but this cup had two good spoonfuls in it at least. It tasted good and it raised a smile.

"That's better, lad."

Joe walked out of the room, and a few seconds later Chris heard the door close. He checked his phone. Ollie might already be awake. He pressed the call button and scrolled down to Lou's number.

It rang several times before Ollie answered it. "Hi, Dad." He sounded sleepy and unhappy.

"Hey, big man. Sleep well?"

"I had an accident."

Ollie had wet the bed again and it always upset him. "That's okay, it's not the end of the world. You'll get the hang of it." He said the same words every time and on each occasion he thought about the year he'd spent waking up in a cold, damp bed.

"But I emptied my tank five times last night." Ollie sounded close to tears.

"Hey, hey, come on, it just takes a little longer for some boys. You'll get there." He didn't like to dwell on it and moved the conversation on. "So, you ready for school?"

He heard Ollie sigh. "It's too early. Mum says I've still got a bit of time left before I need to get dressed."

Of course he did, it wasn't even seven yet. He tried to think about what they usually said to each other in the morning, but that was a natural conversation whereas this felt forced.

"Don't forget your kit, it's football after school tonight, isn't it?"

"That was last year, Dad. This year it's on a Tuesday night because I'm older. I'm a junior." He said the last sentence proudly.

He wanted to reach down the phone and take Ollie in his arms and kiss him. He wanted to say sorry for being absent for the last… he didn't even know how long he'd been absent for. Instead he said, "I love you, Ollie."

"Happy birthday, Dad. I love you too." The reply came back instantly.

"Thanks." He'd forgotten today was his actual birthday. "Okay, well, I'll talk to you later."

"Dad?" Ollie's voice had changed now. He didn't sound sleepy anymore.

"Yes?"

"I think Mum's upset. I heard her crying earlier."

Chris thought of all the times he'd heard his parents arguing and crying. The worst time was when he heard his dad crying. That was the worst sound in the world.

"Is she there?"

"She's in your bedroom. Do you want me to shout her?"

"Please."

He heard the sound of the phone being dropped onto the bed and the muffled sound of Ollie's voice. "Mum!"

There was nothing for a few seconds, then Lou's voice came through. "Hello." Her tone was curt, almost aggressive.

"Morning. Ollie said…"

"I heard him but he's wrong. I wasn't crying, it's hay fever."

Now wasn't the time for an argument. "Okay. Thanks for letting Granddad know I was on my way."

"I didn't want him having a shock in the middle of the night. How is Lollipop?"

"Oh, he's fine. He's gone out for his walk, same as always."

"Okay, well give him my love."

"Will do." There was silence for a moment as both of them tried to find something to say.

"I have to get ready. Happy birthday, Chris."

They said their goodbyes and hung up. It was then that Chris realised he had nothing to do. There was no packed lunch to make or office to retreat to. He was free to do exactly what he wanted. He flopped back down on the bed and drummed his fingers on his chest.

So how exactly do you straighten your head out?

*

He wasn't aware that he'd fallen asleep again until the sound of Joe knocking pots and pans around in the kitchen jolted him awake. His eyes still stung, but if a ninety-one year old was up and about on three hours sleep, then he should be too.

He pulled his jeans and t-shirt on and walked downstairs into the kitchen.

"Morning, again." The table was already set and a fresh mug of tea was waiting for him.

"Sit down, lad. The eggs will be two more minutes."

Chris did as he was told. There was an egg cup on his plate and a thick slice of toast had been cut into strips. Boiled egg and soldiers was another thing he only had when he stayed here.

"How was the walk?" he asked.

"Not bad. The weather's getting worse, but it'll take more than a drop of rain to stop me."

Chris laughed. He had an idea it would take a nuclear

explosion to stop Joe doing anything he set his mind to. He looked out of the window. Blobs of rain had gathered in waxy pools on the bonnet of his car.

"Here you go." Joe spooned an egg into each of their egg cups and sat down. He then poured a generous mound of salt onto his plate.

"Some people reckon you shouldn't eat too much salt, or eggs for that matter, but I've eaten my eggs this way for the last seventy years and look at me."

Chris poured himself some salt and knocked the lid off his egg. "I don't think anyone knows what's good and what's bad anymore."

He plunged a soldier into the egg. The yolk, which was a beautiful orange colour, bubbled over the top. He waited a moment and then bit into it. Why on earth didn't he eat eggs like this at home?

"Good?" Joe asked.

"The best, Granddad. The absolute best." He took a pinch of salt and sprinkled it into the egg. There was no need to say anything else. The food, as simple as it was, was enough. At that moment he knew he had made the right decision to come. There was no question about it.

After much scraping of shells, they both finished their eggs at the same time. Chris wiped his hand across his mouth and finished his tea.

"That was perfect."

Joe pushed his chair back but Chris grabbed his plate before he could stand. "I'll sort these out." He took both plates over to the sink and started running the water.

"I take it the party wasn't a success," Joe asked.

Chris looked out of the window. Beyond his car were only fields. They were empty except for the hedges which gave them a patchwork effect. One tree, which had ceded to the wind and grown at an angle, stood guard in the distance.

"Not exactly." He turned around. "What did Lou say?"

Joe sipped his tea and shrugged. "Nothing other than you were on your way and weren't very good."

"I've started seeing Dad again." There was no point in soft-soaping it, at least not to Joe. "And obviously it's my birthday and I'm now the same age as he was when I…" Joe wouldn't allow him to say the same words he'd used with Lou. "When he died."

Joe reached behind him and pulled open a drawer. He slid an envelope across the table. "You better have this then."

Chris looked at it for a moment. "What is it?"

"Just open it." He sounded serious.

Chris put his finger on the envelope and dragged it toward him. It wasn't a birthday card from Joe, unless he'd changed the habit of a lifetime. Written on the front in faded ink was his name. The gum on the flap had long since dried. He lifted it and removed a folded sheet of paper. He looked at Joe whose expression was inscrutable and then back at the paper again. It was old.

"Should I be sitting down for this?" he asked.

"Probably," Joe replied.

He pulled his chair out and unfolded the paper.

Dear Chris,

I love you. I have always loved you and will always love you. I hope you will be able to forgive me one day.

There are things which you don't understand yet and I hope you never have to try to understand them. Life is difficult and some of us can cope with the decisions we've made and some of us can't. I'm the one who can't.

Please don't blame Mum, it's not her fault.

I'm sorry, I'm sorry, I'm sorry, I'm sorry, I'm sorry.

I love you,
Dad.

Chris stared the last word then turned the paper over in his hand. What was he looking for? An explanation of some sort perhaps? What was he looking at here? He looked at Joe and opened his mouth to speak but he didn't know what to say.

"Your dad wasn't well."

"What?"

"He hadn't been well for a while, Chris. We didn't know what to do, nobody did. Not your mum, nobody."

"He was ill? What kind of ill?" Chris asked the questions but he thought he knew the answer already.

"His mind, his mind was…"

Chris pushed the chair back and threw the note onto the table. "This is a suicide note, isn't it? This is my dad's suicide note to me."

The room started to turn, very slowly at first, but as his breaths became short and rapid, the revolutions grew quicker and quicker until he was forced to grab the edge of the sink to steady himself.

"No," he whispered.

He was aware that Joe had stood up and was coming toward him but he held his hand up. "No," he said, louder this time. Joe stopped in his tracks.

"I'm sorry, son." Maybe when Joe had a cold the tone of his voice might change, but usually it was as steady as a rock. Some might say it was monotonous but Chris thought it reassuring. As he spoke now, Chris heard it falter. He'd never heard it before and it was shocking.

He looked up and saw Joe was holding onto the end of the table. The man had just been on a three mile walk, he didn't need a table to steady himself, not unless he was struggling too.

"He was my boy and I couldn't do anything to help him. Not a thing."

Joe's voice was slipping into the distance, a place that was in the shadows.

"I should've done more to help him but I didn't know what to do. And then you came down here, all of you, for that summer and…"

Chris felt sick. Joe's voice seemed to be coming from another place. It was a place that distorted his words and made them difficult to understand. It sounded like he was speaking through a long cardboard tube that caused dull echoes to form on each and every letter.

He needed to get out of there. He needed to get some air before he puked his guts up all over Joe's kitchen. He staggered to the door and flung it open. He was aware that Joe was shouting at him but his words weren't words anymore, they were just sounds, completely devoid of meaning.

Chapter 5

Chris stumbled onto the lane and started walking. He had no idea where he was going, nor did he care. This wasn't about getting somewhere, this was about getting away from the house. It was about leaving that note behind. Rain lashed his face and exposed arms, and he was vaguely aware of the painful sensation of grit beneath his bare feet. He'd left the house without getting dressed but that wasn't important, not after what he'd just been shown.

He could heard Joe's voice shouting out to him, but as he marched on, the sound retreated into the background and then disappeared entirely. All that was left was the screaming noise of his own thoughts whipping around inside his head. It was deafening and incoherent but above all it was painful; almost too painful.

His dad, the man he had idolised, worshipped and wept over for so many nights and days it was impossible to count, had planned to leave him. The man had written his goodbyes and, if he had been allowed the chance, would have killed himself. And left him.

Like he had left Ollie back at home.

No, no, no, it wasn't the same thing at all. His dad had wanted a permanence to his departure, while all he wanted was a few weeks to get straight so he could return. So he could be a better dad.

But why? Why? Why? Why?

He'd been a good boy, a good son. He'd never got into any trouble, not serious trouble anyway, and he was doing well at school, so why? Why would Dad want to leave him?

Chris stopped walking and looked down. Blood, diluted by the rain, was running off his big toe and onto the lane. He lifted his foot and saw a shard of glass sticking out of the sole. He took it between his fingers and pulled it slowly. Releasing the glass allowed more blood to run from the cut but he pushed his thumb over it and smeared the blood across his foot. The rain would wash it away. The rain was good at doing that.

There was no pain though, no sign that his flesh had been punctured or needed repair, just the faint sensation that walking wasn't as comfortable as it should be. He turned his face to the falling rain. He felt numb all over.

"Dad!" He screamed it at the top of his voice, then he screamed it again and again and again.

*

"I need to know everything and I mean everything." He stood on the doorstep of Joe's cottage. He was soaking wet and cold but he wasn't going in until Joe agreed.

"Come in and get dry, for God's sake."

"Everything."

"Yes, everything. Please, son, come in."

Chris stepped inside and before he could go any farther, Joe flung his arms around him and held him. The old boy was still wiry and strong. Fifty-odd years of mining and fishing did that to a man, but there weren't many of his generation left and there were certainly none as fit as Joe. Nevertheless, his thick sweater couldn't hide the passage of time entirely.

Chris hugged him back. There were questions, lots of questions. Some of them were going to be uncomfortable but for now it was enough that they were united again.

"I'll go and get my bag from the car and get some dry clothes on. Then we're going to talk, Granddad. Okay?"

Joe gently pushed him away. "Best put the kettle on then, eh? Shall we make the coffee Irish?"

Chris nodded. "It's a bit early but I reckon we need it." He turned and walked to the car. He had a feeling they might need everything they drank to be Irish if they were going to get through the next few hours.

Steam rose off the coffee with the familiar spicy scent of Bushmills. If it hadn't been for the envelope which sat on the table between them, it would have been a pleasurable moment. Joe had folded the note back inside during Chris's walk in the rain but the contents were no less obvious.

"So where do you want to start? You know Jack was born and raised down here…"

"The beginning, Granddad," Chris interrupted. "I think I need to start at the beginning." And he did. Being down here had already uncovered something unpleasant and unexpected. He needed to start where it all began.

"Well, your dad was a normal little lad, sometimes good and sometimes naughty but never bad. Good at school, and a pretty decent scrum-half. He had a group of mates and…" Joe paused. "But you're not really interested in that, are you?"

Chris shook his head.

"You want to know what he was actually like, don't you? Your dad was what most people would call shy. I didn't think he was though. He was quiet, yes, but he had a confidence about him that not many people could see and that, at least to me, made him strong." Joe took a drink. He was digging around in a place deep inside that probably hadn't been touched for years.

"When he was a nipper, I used to take him down to Hawk's and sit right at the top of the headland. We'd eat ham sandwiches with English mustard. Those were his favourite. He liked the way the mustard stung his nose and made his eyes water." Joe paused and smiled at the memory. "One day, when we were staring out at the horizon, he asked me if we lived at the edge of the world. I remember it because I recall the look on his face when I told him we didn't. It was as if I'd just taken something away from him. Not a toy or anything, just a bit of mystery, but it was enough to sting."

Chris listened as Joe talked about Jack's younger years. He didn't interrupt him again because they were both lost in thought. Joe stopped periodically to have a drink and to smile or gesticulate about an event, but other than that, the words flowed and the stories weaved in and out of each other. In that hour, Chris heard more about his dad than he had ever done before.

"He missed having a mum of course, we both did, and some of the questions he asked were bloody awful but gradually he stopped asking about her."

"I'm sorry, Granddad, but she left, right? When he was a little boy?"

Joe looked at him and grimaced. "She left when he was really little. She left on the day he was born."

Chris shook his head. "Oh God."

"It's something else I should've told you, I know. She died giving birth to him."

Chris rubbed his hands down his face. "Jesus, Granddad. I…" What could he say? What could he possibly say? The man had lost his wife and his son.

Joe held his hand up. "Old news to me so lets move on."

Chris nodded. It was information which might be relevant later, he knew that, but there was no point in pushing it now.

"Growing up down here is idyllic but it isn't the whole world and Jack wanted more, like most of the kids around here do. They don't know what they've got, in my opinion, but there you go. He wandered off down the road to Exeter University and took his degree. That was a big, big thing back then but he was a clever bugger and he could run rings round the teachers at school. One of them saw it in him and helped him get in. I don't even remember her name now, but we couldn't have done it without her."

Joe was smiling. It was clear how proud he was of his son.

"And that's where he met Sue, your mum. Jack loved her from the moment he clapped eyes on her. Who was I to argue with that? Then they both came down here to live for a year or two after they finished studying. They worked at The Queen's Head in the village for a time while they looked for proper jobs. Looking back on it, I could see all wasn't well with him. I should've pushed them to move out, to get away from here, but I was happy to have him home again." He stopped and looked into his empty cup. "He was thinking too much. I'd catch him sitting where you are now, just staring out of the window. I knew what he was thinking. I knew what he'd been thinking for years but neither of us wanted to say it. I should have, son. I should have said something."

"What was it?"

Joe raised his eyes. "He was thinking something similar to what you've been thinking these past years. He was blaming himself for killing his mum."

They both sat in silence for a while until Joe reached across the table and tapped the envelope. "And I think that was probably at the bottom of this."

Chris looked at the note. "Guilt?"

Joe nodded. "Exactly how you're feeling."

Chris clamped his teeth together until he could feel the tension spread up his jaw and into his temples.

"So when did he write this? When did you find it?"

"I didn't, your mum did. As for when he wrote it, well, it could've been anytime. She found it in his pocket on the day you and him went to Hawk's and she showed it to me. It knocked me sideways, not so much Sue though. She looked like she was expecting it. We had a good heart-to-heart that day and she told me what your dad had been like for the last couple of years. Moody, distant, distracted and he was going missing from work. She thought he was having an affair at first but things started dropping into place. Insomnia, and when he could sleep he had terrible nightmares that left him and the sheets soaking wet. He was ill but he wouldn't let her in, he wouldn't listen to her. She didn't know how to cope with it."

Chris listened with a growing sense of anxiety. He recognised himself in Joe's words. He recognised the moods, the distraction and the insomnia.

"So we decided we were going to talk to him when you got back. We were going to…"

Joe stopped and buried his head in his hands. Chris could hear his breath coming in staggered heaves. He'd never forgotten how it had felt to hear his dad crying and this brought it back. He'd been powerless back then but he wasn't now.

He stood up and walked around the table. Joe wasn't afraid to show affection but he was a strong and proud man, of the generation where tears were not acceptable, particularly not in company. Chris knelt and put his arm around his granddad. There was no need to say a word but the next coffee would definitely need to be Irish again.

*

They both took a deep breath. Chris had made a fresh batch of coffee and laced it with sugar and Bushmills. There was still one last hurdle to jump before Chris had enough information, at least for the time being.

"So that day, whose idea was it for me and Dad to go off together?"

"Oh, that was your dad's. Sue packed you up with sandwiches, ham and mustard because Jack had asked for them, and off you went. I remember the look on your face when you got in the car. You looked like you'd won the football pools. You'd got a couple of quid for ice cream in your pocket too. You were the cat who'd got the cream."

"Dad let me ride in the front seat, I remember that." Chris could almost see his reflection on the car window as he waved to Joe and his mum, grinning like a madman.

"We took the crab-lines down to Bunkers Bay. We never caught a thing but it didn't matter." Chris stopped and bit his lip. "I don't remember Dad being…"

Joe stopped him. "Don't try to put what you know now into that memory. It won't work."

Chris nodded and carried on. "We went to Hawk's Cove and ate our sandwiches in the car. That was Dad's idea but I didn't mind. I was just happy sitting next to him. It wasn't raining but there were grey clouds everywhere." Chris was voicing a memory that was so familiar he could remember every single detail. He'd only ever spoken in such detail three times before though, and it had been several years since the last time. Once to the police, once to Joe and once to Lou. This would be Joe's second time but it needed to be said in the context of all that had preceded it.

"Then we went for a walk along the top of the headland. The waves were incredible. They were frightening and exciting at the same time and I couldn't take my eyes away from them. Dad was staring too but he was looking across the cove and out to the horizon. Before today, I thought he was thinking about what was happening with Mum, about the arguments and about me maybe, but now…" He remembered what Joe had said but ignored it this time. "He was thinking about himself and about the note and his mum. It was probably all going around and around in his head…"

"Stop," Joe said firmly. "There's no point."

It was something he'd think about later but for now he had to leave it alone. "It started raining and Dad gave me a piggyback halfway to the car." He paused and looked at Joe. They both knew where the next bit was heading.

"Then he saw her." He saw Joe flinch but carried on anyway. "On the slipway with the waves crashing around her and on her. God, it was loud. He ran down there and I followed him. I tried to shout but he couldn't hear me and by the time I caught up, he was trying to grab her and pull her out of the sea, back up the slipway. She was shouting at him but the waves were too loud and I couldn't hear what she was saying."

Chris could feel his heartbeat quickening word by word.

"Then Dad was in the sea and it was coming up over his

head. She looked angry, really angry…"

Joe looked away.

"And where her eyes should've been, there was nothing. Nothing except for these great big holes." He took a deep breath and exhaled slowly. "She looked at me, Granddad. She looked at me and said, 'I can see you.' Except it wasn't friendly, it was hideous. How could she see me, though? How could she see me when she didn't have any eyes? How?"

He wasn't after an answer and Joe was looking into his cup anyway.

"I was frightened. She was so horrible that I didn't want to be near her, I didn't want Dad to be near her either so I stepped back and…"

Joe said something but his voice was distorted by the echo in his cup. Chris didn't want to stop to ask what it was though, he needed to finish.

"I think Dad was reaching for me but it seemed I was miles away and he couldn't get to me. And then I was in the water and it was cold. Jesus, it was cold."

"She wasn't there." Joe lifted his head. His words were crystal clear this time. "There was no blind woman, Chris."

The two men stared at each other. They had been through this conversation before.

"When they found you on the slipway, there was nobody there. You were barely alive. You were covered in cuts and bruises, your left arm was broken and you had hypothermia. Your mum screamed when she saw you. All of those things are true, all of those things happened but that woman did not exist. She wasn't there, son."

"I saw…"

"The police couldn't find her and nobody in the village had ever seen a woman who looked like that. If you want to get yourself sorted out, you've got to stop. For Ollie, you have to stop. You have to stop feeling guilty and you have to stop talking about this blind woman. It was an accident, just a terrible, terrible accident and that's what you've got to accept."

That was what it boiled down to, at least according to the police – a terrible and unfortunate accident. Father and son in Hawk's Cove, hit by a wave and dragged into the Atlantic. Son rescued by father who was unable to save himself. A terrible accident but case closed.

The police, his mum and Joe had told him the same thing over and over again. He even heard one of the officers tell his mum that he'd made it up as a coping mechanism. To help him come to terms with it and to assuage any guilt.

Well, if he had made her up, why did he still feel guilty? Why could he see her face clearer than he could see his dad's? He was confused about a lot of things but he wasn't confused about her. She had been there.

There was no way Joe would accept it though.

He dragged the note across the table. "Who else knows about this?" He hoped this would distract Joe.

"Just the three of us now."

Chris nodded. "You didn't show the police?"

"Why would we? What happened had nothing to do with what he'd written."

"And you didn't think it would be something I'd need to

know about sooner?"

Joe shook his quickly. "No, of course not. I... we... decided there was no reason for you to ever know about it. What good would it have done?"

"Well..." Chris began and then stopped. He couldn't think of a reason to argue.

"It wouldn't have done any good." Joe looked down at the note. "I'm not sure I made the right decision now but with what Lou told me, it seemed like it was the right time."

"What exactly did she say?"

"That you were becoming like your dad. She didn't say that of course, but what she said was exactly what your mum went through with Jack." He reached over and grabbed the note. "I don't want you writing something like this to Ollie." He stuffed the letter inside his pocket. "I'll get rid of this later. There's no reason to keep it now."

Neither of them spoke for a while. The only sounds were the occasional click from the fridge and rain splashing against the window. The noises were hypnotic but they were quiet compared with the sound of the thoughts crashing about in Chris's head. They smashed into each other like waves on the cliffs at Hawk's Cove and it was deafening. Right in the centre of all of them was the immovable image of a woman. A blind woman with an ugly voice and terrifying dark holes where her eyes should have been.

She was there. Oh yes, she had always been there

Chapter 6

Chris said goodnight to Ollie and ended the call. Lou had managed a few words but she sounded tired, and although she was trying to sound positive, he could tell she didn't feel that way. He hadn't mentioned the note or his conversation with Joe. She hadn't asked how he was doing, but he supposed she'd been asking that question for so long and received nothing but monosyllabic responses that she'd simply given up.

He thought about it for a moment. Maybe he should have offered the information without being asked? But then did she really need to know at this very moment? He knew the answer to that. Whatever came out of this time, down here with Joe, they would speak about it later when they were together again. Because they would be together again, he knew that too; all three of them.

Joe had gone out after dinner. He'd walked into the village for his nightly game of dominoes at the pub. He said he wouldn't go, it being Chris's birthday, but Chris had waved him away. His birthday was the last thing on his mind, besides he knew how much it meant to Joe. Chris had offered to take him but he'd refused the offer, stating proudly that he always walked and the day he couldn't manage the three mile round-trip would be the same day they put him in the ground. Chris knew better than to argue and he was happy to be on his own for a few hours. Joe wouldn't leave the pub until closing time, until he'd finished his second pint of Tribute and taken a few quid from the other old boys.

He tapped the screen on his phone a few times and looked at the screensaver. It was a picture of him, Lou and Ollie on their last week here just over a year ago. Ollie was in the middle and he was holding a crab by its leg. It was the only time they had managed to catch anything during the whole week and that was because Joe had been with them.

He smiled and put the phone in his pocket. It usually took him three or four days to get used to the silence but it seemed especially loud tonight. He got up from the kitchen table and walked past the stairs, into the small sitting room. There was a small television in the corner, which Joe had only bought to satisfy Ollie, plus a two-seater and an armchair. Neither chairs looked to have been used very much.

He stood on the threshold and looked in. The last time they came, Ollie had moaned about the lack of channels on the box. Joe had clapped him on the back and told him he wouldn't have much time for watching it so it didn't matter.

He was right too and Ollie hadn't missed his daily ration of cartoons in the slightest. How could he? He was too busy learning how to surf and trying to catch crabs.

It had been a great holiday but even then he could feel the year creeping up on him with unchallenged certainty. Lou had felt it too. Undoubtedly.

Things had changed since then and not just the subtle mood change, thought process and general despondency which became part of his daily wake-up ritual. No, all of those things had joined together in a grim recipe and made a new human. It was someone he barely recognised. And something new was changing too. He hadn't quite come to terms with it yet but there was going to be a change in how he felt about his dad.

He was still his hero but as well as having a flaw, there was now a crack which ran down the length of his memory. It wasn't very wide but Chris knew if he pulled back the edges and peered inside, he might see a fragment of his own reflection in there. He wasn't prepared to look inside yet.

He looked across the room toward the bookcase. It was dark but the moon shone brightly through the hazy coastal clouds. He could see the faint outline of three photo-frames on the shelf. He knew what was in them all. One was Joe and his Lizzy on their wedding day; one was Ollie, Lou and himself; and the other was a picture of Joe and Jack together. He stared at the dark square for a moment and in his mind's eye, he could see the photograph clearly. Father and son together. Jack in his early twenties, back from university for a few weeks, and Joe beside him. They were both laughing about something, probably one of Joe's bad jokes, and in the background was… What exactly was in the background? He couldn't remember where the photograph had been taken because he'd only ever focused on the two men in the foreground.

He stepped into the room and the faint but pleasant aroma of a real fire greeted him. The fire hadn't been on since the winter but the smell never left the room. It permeated every stick of furniture and every carpet fibre.

He pulled the frame down and held it in his hands.

The two men were little more than shadows but Chris closed his eyes and ran his fingers over each of their forms in the hope it would make them come to life in his mind. The image was black and white but he knew his dad's chestnut hair held none of the grey flecks it had later in life, like his own now did. Joe's thick hair had been silver for as long as he'd known him. They both had dimples on either side of their thin-lipped mouths. Joe's face was a little rounder than Jack's but other than that, there was no disputing they were father and son.

He traced their outlines, lingering a little longer on his father's form before moving away from them. There was landscape of some sort in the background rather than a man-made structure, he recalled that much, but as for where it was…

An electric shock, or what felt like one, charged up his finger and into his brain. It exploded in a blinding flash and in that moment she was there again. She was inside his head and her eyes were like the gateways to hell.

"I can see you!" Her voice was deafening.

Chris opened his eyes and let go of the frame. It hit the floor with a dull thud. Even though his eyes were open, the image was burned onto his retinas and he could still see her floating in front of him.

"No," he whispered, breaking free of the paralysis that was rooting him to the spot. He rubbed his eyes, shook his head, and little by little she faded away.

He took several deep breaths and looked down at the frame. It was just tiredness and stress playing games with him, he knew that, but it had been intense and he found himself not wanting to touch the photograph again.

"Get a grip." He spoke louder this time but it didn't sound confident at all.

He knelt down and looked at it. The moon lit the two men like a spotlight on stage. They looked so happy together. Joe had his arm around Jack's shoulder and they were both grinning wildly. He couldn't see the dimples on their cheeks but he knew they were there, the camera just hadn't been good enough to pick them up.

He'd been right about the background. There was nothing except fields behind them. The picture had probably been taken just behind the cottage by his mum. He might have to ask Joe about it tomorrow. He reached out and picked it up. He tutted at himself when there was no replay of what had just happened, stood up quickly and put the frame back before it could. As he reached forward to replace it, moonlight flashed across the picture, illuminating the edge of the photograph. Was that someone standing behind them? He brought it closer. It looked like someone…

A loud bang on the window beside his head almost caused him to drop the frame again. He looked up and saw a shadow moving about outside. It moved around the side of the house and was followed by a loud bang on the back door. His heart rate had only just slowed down from the incident a couple of minutes ago and now it was racing again.

"You in there?"

He recognised the voice immediately and his heartbeat started to slow.

"On my way!" he shouted out. As he lifted the frame to replace it again, he took one last look. There was nobody else in it, of course there wasn't. There never had been, it was just a trick of the light. He shot an accusatory glance at the moon and put it back next to the photograph of Joe and Lizzy on their wedding day. He needed a decent night's sleep but he got the feeling he might need the help of Joe's Irish pal Mr Bushmills to help him with that tonight.

*

"Joe told me you were here." Pat Bailey stood on the doorstep with a big, stupid grin on his face and a Co-op carrier bag in his fist. "I've bought your favourite." He lifted the carrier bag and shook it to emphasise his point.

Chris laughed, glad of the company. "Good to see you, Pat." He stepped aside to let him in but Pat grabbed him by the shoulders.

"You look more and more like your old man every time

I clap eyes on you." He stepped inside and put the bag on the table. Chris could smell the pub on his breath but he an idea that was how Pat smelled most days.

"You here for long then?" Pat was already opening cupboard doors looking for glasses.

"They're in that one." Chris pointed at one of the cupboards and opened the carrier bag. Inside was a box containing twelve bottles of Cornish Rattler.

"We don't have to drink it all." Pat put two glasses on the table. "We can leave one for Joe." He patted Chris on the back, opened the bottles, handed one to Chris and chinked them together. "Cheers. Not sure why I got the glasses though." He took a long drink straight from the bottle and sat down.

"Come on then, what's happening?" Pat asked.

Pat had always been like this. He was a force of nature. He had also been his dad's best friend when they were growing up and had been best man at his wedding. He had spent a lot of time in Joe's cottage as a boy and Joe considered him part of the family; a son, his only son now. Pat had none of his own family and had never found a woman who was willing to put up with him, but that never seemed particularly high on his agenda.

Chris took a sip. He hadn't tasted cider for over a year and it had never been a favourite, but for some reason Pat thought it should be.

"Not much," he lied. "I've just come down to see Granddad for a few days. A bit of a break."

Pat nodded and drained the bottle. "Well, it's your

birthday today so drink up." He wiped a grubby hand across his bearded chin and slid another bottle toward Chris.

He caught the bottle but had barely started on the first. "What about you?"

"Same old. Still doing a bit from time to time but I've hung up the lobster pots. Sarah-Jane got sold to some idiot over in Penzance." He rubbed his chin again. "But you know that bit."

Sarah-Jane had been Joe's boat and it would have been passed on to Jack, had he been interested. Instead, Pat took it on when Jack moved away. Pat had asked Chris to buy it off him when he retired but Chris wanted nothing to do with it, so he'd been forced to sell it to someone else. This had been nearly two years ago but it was clearly something Pat thought worth mentioning again.

"Give it up, Pat. Can you imagine me in a boat? Sarah-Jane would've been smashed to bits by now. It's better off with someone who knows what they're doing." Chris left out the bit about how just looking at the sea scared the hell out of him.

"You could've had it for your lad. I bet *he'd* love to go out."

"Oh well," Chris replied. He wanted this conversation to be over and his response was purposefully bland. There was no way he would allow Ollie anywhere near a boat.

They both lifted their bottles and took a drink. This time Chris finished his bottle and opened the next.

"That's more like it." Pat laughed and started peeling the label off his bottle. "Your dad loved a scrumpy." He pulled the label off completely and rolled it between his fingers. "And he could drink a bit too. In his younger days, he could drink me under the table."

Chris smiled. The more Pat drank, the more wistful he usually became and although the stories tended to be the same ones, they were safe. Pat opened one bottle after another in a continual stream. It was as impressive as it was depressing.

"We got into some bother, your dad and me. It's a wonder Joe's got any hair left with all the grief we caused him. Jack had a grey Hillman Minx and the year before he went up to Exeter, we were kings. We went everywhere in that car, sometimes with a couple of other lads in the back and sometimes, if we were lucky, a couple of girls, but mostly just the two of us. I remember the summer just before he went off. We were both supposed to be helping Joe with his pots but I don't remember a lot of work going on. I certainly don't remember too many early starts. We did enough to pay for a tank of petrol, a couple of pints and a packet of Embassy between us. Then off we'd go, just driving around, up and down the coast, filling the car with smoke and meaningless bollocks. We were kings. We were invincible."

Pat stopped talking and Chris saw a flash of something pass over his face. Was it grief, pain or just old age? He was seventy-three years old, the same age his dad would have been.

"Have you been up to see him yet?" Pat asked.

"Not yet," Chris replied. "I'll go up tomorrow." What had been left of his dad, when they found him, was buried in the cemetery just outside the village. He hadn't gone the last time they were here but Lou had gone with Joe and put flowers down. He'd ask Joe to go with him tomorrow. He could visit Lizzy at the same time. He finished another bottle and put it down. The alcohol was speeding through his blood, making him feel tired.

"Listen Pat, I'm..."

Pat stood up and downed another bottle. He belched loudly and said, "I know, Joe told me not to keep you up." He looked at his watch. "If I'm quick I can make it back for last orders."

Chris walked to the door and opened it. "Good to see you, Pat. Take care of yourself."

Pat stepped outside and turned. "He loved you. He really loved you."

Chris nodded and with that Pat walked away. He held his arm up and shouted over his shoulder as he disappeared into the darkness. "I'll see you before you go, lad."

Chris shouted back. "Take it easy, Pat!"

He closed the door and looked at the dozen empty bottles on the table. He'd had three so somehow Pat had managed to drink nine bottles. It looked like Pat's drinking had gone to a different level. He very much doubted whether his dad could drink Pat under the table now. He doubted whether anyone in the village could.

He cleared the bottles off the table and stared at the balled-up labels Pat had pulled off. He hadn't seemed to get any pleasure from the cider, it was just one bottle after another until they were gone and then so was he. It was just coincidence that Chris had called time because Pat would have been leaving anyway. If the man wasn't an alcoholic, he was as close as possible. There was no way his dad would have become like this. No way.

He yawned. Joe didn't need anyone waiting up for him and he was exhausted anyway. The cider might just have done the trick. He left the kitchen light on and walked upstairs to bed. Tomorrow he would go with Joe to put some flowers down and maybe have a walk around the village. The tourists would be long gone so it would be quiet.

Things had changed today. He'd never held resentment for his mum, that was too strong an emotion to describe how he felt, but there had always been a feeling that she was in some way to blame for how distant his dad grew toward the end. She wasn't to blame at all, he knew that now. It was quite the opposite. She had tried to help and support him.

Nobody had told him about the note. Not because they wanted to keep it a secret but because they wanted him to hold onto his dad as a hero, and not someone for whom life was too much. Chris lay in the darkness and listened to a fox screeching in the distance. There was still so much he didn't know about the man. Things he would probably never know now, but as painful as it had been to see the suicide note, it made a horrible sense. It completed a missing part of the jigsaw. The picture wasn't just of his dad, it was also of himself.

He closed his eyes and let sleep drag him away from his thoughts. He didn't have the energy to think about it tonight. And he certainly didn't have the strength to keep pushing the image of the woman away; the woman with eye sockets that led straight to hell. She was in his head now and for some reason she wanted to be involved.

Chapter 7

Chris had already started boiling water for the eggs when Joe got back from his walk. Joe looked startled when he walked through the door.

"Morning." He looked straight at the pan. He was very particular about the consistency of the yolk and Chris had no intention of disappointing him.

He lowered the eggs into the water and started the timer on his mobile. "Five minutes, Granddad, and not a second more."

"Good lad." Joe sat down at the table.

Chris turned his attention away from the eggs. "I was thinking we could go up and see Dad this morning?"

"You want to go up there?" He sounded surprised.

"I think I need to. I think it'd be good for me," Chris said. Joe's expression was difficult to read. "Unless you've got something else on? We could go…"

"No, no, that's fine by me. I'll pick some violets from the

garden for Lizzy."

Chris popped the bread down in the toaster and poured the tea. Joe looked tired this morning but that wasn't surprising since he was over ninety and had been out until way after Chris had fallen asleep. He had to hand it to the man, he was as fit as a fiddle. Joe added, "And tonight I'll let you drive me up to The Queen's. It's curry night, my treat for your birthday. Two for a tenner."

"Sounds good." He turned around. "Pat came round last night. He was half-cut by the time he got here."

Joe slurped his tea and sighed. "That lad likes his pop a bit too much. He's a worry."

Chris took the eggs out of the water and put them into cups. "Well, he put nine bottles of Rattler away while he was here. He was like a factory." He quickly buttered the toast and put the plates down on the table.

Joe looked at his plate. "That better still be runny." He picked up his spoon and knocked the head off the egg. "Not bad."

They ate their breakfast in silence. Chris looked up once or twice for a sign from Joe. It was only a boiled egg but it wasn't as tasty as one of Joe's.

*

Chris drove slowly up the lane toward the village. The telephone conversation with Ollie and Lou had been fraught. There was no animosity from Lou but she was clearly struggling. Ollie had wet the bed again and was upset about it, but he'd also been up two or three times in the night crying. Lou told him that on the second occasion, Ollie walked into their room screaming. He'd been in a trance or sleepwalking and when she'd finally managed to get through to him, he wouldn't go back in his own bed for a long time.

Chris felt terrible. He felt selfish and guilty but above all he felt like a failure. He said he was driving home immediately, and he'd meant it too, but Lou had told him that if he did she would take Ollie to her parents' house. Was this how it had been between his mum and dad? He didn't remember wetting the bed, but then again his dad had been there, sort of. He'd been in the house at least.

He shook the thoughts away and pressed down on the pedal. He felt better than he had on the night he'd arrived but where was this all heading? There was no miracle cure hidden away under the floorboards in Joe's cottage. Although Joe had some answers, he didn't have them all.

He looked over at Joe in the passenger seat. He admired him more than anyone else he knew. The old man had been dealt the worst hand imaginable but it hadn't stopped him. Losing a wife and then a son was an unimaginable hell that nobody should have to live through, and yet he had. He hadn't allowed himself the luxury of running away either, he'd just got on with life.

"Eyes on the road," Joe said quietly.

The lane wound its way through the fields like a snake. The hedges on either side were as high as a man and although they looked like they were made of gorse, beneath them was a hard stone wall. Many a tourist had found out the hard way when they tried to make room for a car coming the opposite direction.

"So how many books have you written now?" Joe asked.

Chris inhaled deeply and let his breath out slowly. He didn't really want to talk about his books or writing. "Well, there are five out there at the moment and two more with the editor." Joe had started it all off. His tales about King Arthur were at the root of all Chris's writing, or what he used to write before this year kicked in.

Joe nodded. "Have I got them all?"

Chris smiled, despite the topic of conversation. "I sent you a copy of each one. Haven't you read them?" In each of the books, Chris had put *Thanks Granddad!* in the acknowledgements.

Joe laughed. "Nope, not one. There's enough horror out there." He pointed at the road in front. "When are you going to write a proper book?"

Chris laughed now. "A proper book?"

"You know, a thriller. A proper book."

"Just read the first few pages, Granddad, that's all I ask."

They drove past the first row of houses that signalled the start of the village. Most of them were either second homes or holiday lets, which at this time of the year were empty. It made this part of the village seem like a ghost town. Chris drove slowly through the centre, past The Queen's Head and the closed antique shops, out of the other side. It was just after nine and the village was dead. In the summer months there would be a queue of people outside the bakery waiting for fresh bread and croissants. The Co-op would be busy with people buying bacon to make sandwiches to eat outside their tents and caravans. Just over a month had passed since the summer holidays ended but it was like a different place entirely.

They passed more houses on the way up the hill, then the view opened up again. Dotted across the fields were the remnants of the tin-mining industry. Ollie thought they were castles the first time he'd seen them which prompted Joe into one of his stories about Arthur. Just like Chris had done at the same age, Ollie sat open-mouthed and wide-eyed while listening to Joe's tales.

The road carried straight on toward Penzance but Chris took a right turn onto a minor road. He could count on his hand the number of times he had actually been inside the cemetery. It was a good deal fewer than the number of times he'd sat in the car on the lane outside, willing himself to go in.

As they pulled to a stop, he left his hands on the steering wheel. Now they were here, he found himself wishing he was somewhere else.

Joe put his hand on top of his. It was cold.

"I think you've got a lot you need to say to him. I'll pop and see Lizzy and then walk back to the village. We need some more eggs."

Chris looked at him and nodded. "Okay." Joe was right, as usual.

They climbed out of the car and Joe opened the cemetery gate. He was clutching a small bunch of violets to leave on his wife's grave. The flowers shook in his hand. Chris was immediately taken back to the day they brought his dad up here in a coffin and stopped on the threshold. He had been blind on that day, such was the flow of tears. And when they lowered his ruined body into the ground, he felt something snap inside his head. Whatever it was had stopped him speaking for more than a week. Whatever it was, was still partly broken.

"Come on." Joe waited for him.

They walked side by side along the path. There was a small building by the side of the entrance, little more than the size of a shed. It served as a store and probably a waiting room but its dilapidated condition was an indication of obsolescence. Chris remembered how bright the building's whitewash had been on that day. It had pierced his blurred vision and made a sun where the real one was covered by cloud.

On either side of the path, there were neat rows of headstones. Some were covered in lichen and unreadable, some were made of the glossy black marble that made them impossible to age. They knew where they were going, though. The exact location had been scorched into their brains. Even blindfolded and dizzy, they could have walked straight there without missing a step.

Joe removed his cap and crouched to place the violets on his wife's grave. It was a little overgrown and remnants of rotten bunches of flowers were scattered on the earth. They were brown and lifeless beside the vibrant dark purple of Joe's fresh bunch.

Joe kissed the tip of his forefinger and touched the top of

the black headstone. He said nothing for a moment and just stared at the golden letters. Chris stared too. Next to Lizzy Kestle, his grandmother, was his dad and he didn't want to look at him just yet. It seemed that the whole world was silent. He couldn't hear the birds or even the hum of traffic on the main road. The cemetery was cut off from the world which was exactly how he felt at that moment.

"I've bought your boy up to see you, Jack." Joe's voice broke the silence and he touched Chris on the arm.

"Go steady, lad, and I'll see you later." Joe kissed his finger again and touched his son's headstone. He squeezed Chris's arm and walked away. Was that a slight limp? No, it couldn't be, the man was rock-steady, yet he was over ninety so it shouldn't be a surprise. Chris watched him walk away.

As Joe closed the gate, he touched the brim of his cap as if he were signalling someone; as if he were saying, *'Good morning.'*

Chris smiled, but something moved on the edge of his vision and jolted him. He was sure something had shifted beside the little building. He hadn't seen anyone and there was no sign that any animals were here. And yet something dark had flickered on the periphery of his sight. There had been movement; rapid, sharp movement. He stared at the shed and listened. The only sounds were Joe's footsteps and they were retreating into the distance rapidly.

"Hello?" It was probably just a crow. There was nothing and nobody here except him. Except of course for his dad, his long-dead dad. He turned and looked at the headstone. It was black, just like Lizzy's.

"Jack Kestle." His voice sounded like it had been turned up to ten on the volume dial.

"Dad." He'd said the word many times before, many, many times. Now it felt different. He was looking at the place where the body of his dad had been left and he was calling him that word. He hadn't said that to him since he'd been scared out of his wits by a woman who nobody else believed was there.

"I'm sorry, Dad. I'm sorry I fell in. I'm sorry because it's my fault you had to save me, you had to fetch me out and… and…" He could feel the tears flowing down his cheeks and his voice shaking but he wanted to carry on. If he stopped now, how would he ever start again?

"But why did you go down there? Why did you go down there to her? I followed you, I had to follow you but it wasn't safe, Dad, it wasn't safe and we shouldn't have gone. Why? Why? Why?" He banged his fists on the top of the headstone.

"We shouldn't have been there!" His voice came in ragged sobs but there was anger too. He hadn't expected it to be so strong, so close to the surface.

"You were going to leave me. Granddad showed me the note. You were going to leave me. You were going to leave me!" He was close to erupting. He wanted to rip the headstone out of the ground and smash it to pieces with his bare hands. He wanted to jump up and down on it until the bones in his feet were in a thousand pieces. Mostly though, he wanted to dig six feet down and take the skeleton from the coffin and… And what?

It was his fault. It was all his fault that his dad was down there in the box. He'd put him there. He fell to his knees and grabbed the shoulders of the cold granite. "I want you here. I need you!" He could no longer see the words on the stone through the tears in his eyes. It was as it had been on the day he was buried. "I need you, Dad."

Agonising cramp was the only thing which finally forced him to move. Both of his arms trembled but his right forearm bulged as the muscle tightened and went into spasm. He rubbed it furiously and fell back on his haunches. His dad wasn't to blame and neither was he. He knew that really, he knew it deep, deep down, but the guilt was there, it would always be there. To blame someone was easy, even if it was yourself.

He rubbed his eyes and wiped his face on his sleeve. There would be no more tears. She was to blame, she had always been to blame.

He looked at his dad's name on the stone. "I saw her, Dad. I saw you trying to help her but they all said I made her up. They all think you killed yourself and I made her up to help me cope."

Chris stood up and bit his lip. "I know you didn't, though. I know she was there."

There it was again. That flicker on the edge of his vision. He snapped his head around and looked to his left and then to his right. There was nothing except for rows of graves and withered flowers. His eyes were just sore from the tears.

He put his hand back on the stone. "I did see her."

"And I see you."

He dropped his hand and turned around. A shadow, a jet-black shadow, slid across the front of the shabby shed. It clung to the dirty whitewash as if it were crawling. He stared open-mouthed. It stopped, just for a moment, and subtly changed shape. *She* was here. It was as if she were looking directly at him. The moment seemed to last for an age, then she slipped around the side of the building and was gone.

A cloud maybe? He looked up. There were clouds, the sky was full of them; so full that there was no sun to cast a shadow.

He looked at the shed. What was he expecting to see? There was nothing except for some fading graffiti and a green stain under the water tap. He shook his head and turned back to the headstone. Something had changed again. He had vented his anger, frustration and grief before. As a child he'd spoken to the counsellors his mum had arranged. He'd tried three of them before she realised they weren't helping him.

He'd spoken to Joe too. And that had worked, at least on some level. But this was different. He now stood in front of his dad saying the things he'd needed to say to him for the last thirty-three years. Why hadn't he done it sooner?

He knew the answer to that. He was frightened. He knew if he came here, he would start blaming his dad for what happened. He would blame him for going down into the cove, down onto the slipway, and for trying to help someone. He didn't want that. Jack Kestle was a hero, he was a man who died saving his son from drowning. He hadn't made a mistake. He hadn't put them both at risk. He wasn't to blame. It was easier to blame himself. Chris Kestle had killed his own father.

And yet now that had changed. At least some of it had changed. Jack Kestle had chosen to go down into the cove and try to save a complete stranger. Jack Kestle had chosen to do that in the same way as he'd chosen to write a goodbye note to his son. Jack Kestle wasn't to blame and neither was Chris Kestle. *She* was to blame.

He kissed his forefinger, just as Joe had done, and touched the top of the stone.

"I'll find her, Dad. I'll find her."

Chapter 8

"If you're buying the food then I'm paying for the drinks. Okay?" Chris pulled into The Queen's Head car park.

Joe reached for the door handle without saying anything.

"I'm not going in if you don't let me."

Joe sighed and tapped his jacket pocket. "I'm not destitute yet. I can still afford to treat my grandson to a pint now and again."

"I know you can but fair's fair and it's my round. Agreed?"

Joe grunted and opened the door. "If you're buying, I'll have a *pint* of Tribute then."

Chris climbed out. He felt better than he had for a very long time. He was ravenous and Joe had given the curry a very good review on the drive into the village, particularly the effect it had on his digestive system.

Joe led the way and walked straight into the rear of the pub. It was like a cave; a place you might expect to find a smuggler hunched over a table with a purse of doubloons. There was a snug where Joe would probably meet his friends later for dominoes, and a lounge where families and tourists went. Candle-shaped lights, complete with fake dripping wax, gave the room a gloomy, orange glow.

When Lou and Ollie were with him, they rarely came to the pub. Instead, they would buy fish and chips and take them to Cape Cornwall for a picnic. It was Ollie's favourite and if he was given the choice he would eat that every night, or they might buy warm pasties and eat them in the village square. Ollie loved that too because Lou allowed him to go on his own and buy an ice cream from the shop on the other side of the square. She watched him like a hawk every step of the way though. They both did.

"We'll sit there." Joe pointed to a table at the bottom of the room, closest to the fire. It wasn't lit, but in another month or so the room would be glowing with real flames, not the fake electric ones on the wall. Joe liked to eat early so they were the only people in the room.

"And I'll have chicken jalfrezi with a naan and extra poke." He wandered off toward the table.

"Poke?" Chris called out after him.

Joe waved his hand in the air. "She knows what I mean."

"He means extra chillies."

Chris turned and looked into the face of a smiling middle-aged woman. "He always has extra poke with his jalfrezi."

"Sooner him than me," Chris said. He quickly scanned the menu on the bar. "I'll go for the lamb bhuna please, with a naan as well."

"No poke?"

"I'll leave it this time, thanks. Can we have two Tributes too, please?"

She started pulling the beer. "You're Jack's lad, aren't you?"

Chris nodded. "Yep." Inside, he groaned.

She put one of the drinks on the bar. "He was in the year above me at school. Nice lad."

He never knew quite what to say in these situations. "Thanks."

She stared at him as she pulled the other pint. He smiled but it felt uncomfortable, as if she were examining him.

She finished and put the pint down. "You've got the same eyes."

Chris paid her and she walked off toward the kitchen. How close had she got to his dad to know they had the same eyes? He shook his head, stuffed the change in his pocket. Joe had taken his jacket off and had already pushed the napkin into his collar. He wore a shirt every single day, not always with a tie but he'd worn one at the cemetery earlier.

Chris put the drinks on the table and sat down. "Cheers!" He held his glass up.

"Here's to you. Happy birthday, son."

They chinked glasses and took a drink. He loved it when Joe called him son or lad. It made him feel connected to both Joe and his dad.

The shadow at the cemetery had been bothering him all day, even more so than the photograph frame incident. That had come from fatigue and stress, nothing more. He could explain what happened at the cemetery in the same way but the shadow on the shed wall wasn't a trick of his eyesight, he was sure. The way it crept across the wall was… revolting. It turned his stomach just thinking about it.

"Do you believe in ghosts?" He put his glass down and looked at Joe. He had an idea what the answer to his question might be.

"Yep," he answered immediately.

It caught Chris off guard. He'd been expecting a response containing the words 'stupid' or 'ridiculous' or maybe something even stronger, not a straightforward 'yes'.

"You do?" He looked into Joe's eyes for a sign he was being mocked, especially now he knew how Joe felt about the genre of his writing. He could see none.

"Of course I do. I think anyone who doesn't is a fool."

Chris remained silent. He still wasn't entirely sure whether he was being teased.

Joe took a drink and winked. "They keep a good pint."

"Are you taking the mickey?"

Joe shook his head. "I see Lizzy every time I go up there. She's waiting."

"Waiting?" Chris asked. He was sure Joe wasn't teasing him now.

"Waiting for me. At least that's what I think anyway. Waiting and watching. Watching over her boy. The son she never met. Anyway, she looks happy enough up there so I don't see any harm in it."

Chris took a moment and thought about the shadow that

dragged itself across the cemetery store.

"And what does she look like?"

Joe took another drink. "At this rate, I'll need another one of these before my dinner." He put his glass down. "She looks just like she always has done in here." He tapped his forehead with his finger. "On the day we met. Beautiful."

"And is that who you tipped your hat to this morning?"

"Yes. Yes it was. I think maybe I'm being broken in, nice and steady like."

"What do you mean?"

Joe picked his drink up again. "Well maybe, just maybe, when you get to my age you start seeing a few things you never thought you'd see. The layer between us and them gets a bit thinner and you're given a little peek through now and again. Just so that when you go it isn't quite as much of a shock. Give me another couple of years and I'll be seeing Lord Nelson and Queen Victoria wandering around in the square over there."

They both sat in silence for a minute. Chris could find no hole in Joe's logic.

"Here it is!" Joe grabbed his knife and fork. "I hope there's extra poke in there."

The waitress delivered the food in two visits and it smelled incredible. Chris could smell the chilli in Joe's jalfrezi but he tucked in with gusto. There was even a whole red chilli on top which he ate first. He devoured it as if he were eating an apple.

Joe looked up briefly. "How's yours?"

Chris took a mouthful of lamb which melted like butter

on his tongue. "Lovely. Yours?"

"Spiky." He wiped his mouth with the napkin. Chris could see a few beads of sweat on his forehead.

"Looks it."

They ate the rest of the meal in a comfortable silence. It didn't last long because Joe ate his as fast as he ate his boiled egg.

"You can't stop eating to talk. The moment you do that, it gets you." Joe untucked his napkin, wiped his mouth and scrunched it into a ball. He dropped it onto his empty plate.

"That filled you, lad?"

Chris still had a few mouthfuls to go and even though he was full he wasn't about to leave any. "Just a bit. It's tasty, really tasty."

Joe reached into his jacket and slid a ten pound note across the table. "My treat."

Chris opened his mouth but Joe spoke before he could. "No arguing. And when you're done I'll have a half, please." He drained his glass and patted his belly. His cheeks glowed red and he looked healthy.

The meal had provided a natural break in the conversation and Chris had no intention of raising ghosts again. The pub was filling up. Most of those arriving knew Joe and came over to talk to him. They all shook hands with Chris and some, but not all, mentioned his dad. At just before eight o'clock, Joe stood up.

"I'm going to play dominoes with the boys. I'll happily walk home if you've had enough."

Chris looked around the pub. He didn't know anyone enough to talk to but he didn't fancy being alone in the cottage.

"I'll stay for a bit and watch you, if that's okay? I'm just going to phone Ollie."

"Course it is." Joe set off toward the snug and Chris followed with the drinks. The little room was empty but a box of dominoes and a reserved sign had been put in the middle of the table. There was no disputing whose territory this was. How many smugglers had sat on the very same wooden benches?

Chris set the drinks down and walked outside to phone Ollie. The air was fresh and cool. In the distance he could hear the sound of the waves crashing into Hawk's Cove. It made him shiver but he discarded the image of the cove from his mind easily. He'd been doing that same thing for most of his life.

Ollie spoke about his day at school and what he'd had for dinner, but he seemed distracted.

"What's the matter?" Chris asked.

"I don't want to go to bed."

"Come on, Ollie, you've got to go to bed. You need to get your batteries recharged for tomorrow."

"I don't want to, Dad."

"Well if you don't got to bed, I'm going to phone school and tell Mrs Simpson…"

"I'm scared."

Chris cringed. He should be there. "Of what, big boy? Your bed is the safest place in the whole…"

"Of the nightmares." Ollie's voice was shaking.

"They're not real. It's just your mind playing a nasty trick, that's all. I bet you have some good dreams too?" He was a fine one to talk about tricks of the mind. His own mind was in a shambles.

"But they are real, Dad."

"Have you talked to Mum about them?"

There was silence on the other end. Chris was desperately thinking of something to say. "Want to come and see Lollipop and go surfing?"

"When?" Ollie's voice changed in an instant and it made Chris smile.

"Well, I'll talk to Mum but it's half-term in a week or so."

"Yes, yes, yes!" Ollie shouted.

"Well, think about that when you're going off to sleep and you'll be fine. Just think about eating fish and chips down at the cape."

"I will."

"Okay, off you go. Night, night. I love you. Can you put Mum on please?"

"She's in the shower. I love you too, night night."

Chris was about to end the call but stopped. "Ollie?"

"Yes?"

"You can phone me anytime you want, you know that right? Even if it's the middle of the night and you're scared, just tell Mum you want to speak to me. Okay?"

"Okay. You know when we come to see Lollipop, can we go to that place where he caught the crab? I think I know how to catch one now. I'm going to catch the big mutant crab that he told me about. I don't want to eat it though, not like Lollipop. He likes eating crabs but I don't."

Chris laughed. Ollie was already thinking about coming here. That was good.

"Of course we can, we'll go and find this super-crab and then Lollipop can eat him. We're going to need a new crab-line though, especially if it's that big. Tell Mum I'll text her later."

"Night!" He sounded happy again.

Ollie ended the call before he could say anything else. He stood for a moment. Beside the low hum of the waves and the chatter of people in the pub, he could hear his own heart beating loud and clear. He felt stronger too. The thing that had broken on the day they buried his dad wasn't fixed. He doubted it ever would be, but today he'd pushed a tiny bit of glue into one of the cracks. He just hoped it was superglue and not paste.

Chris went to watch the old boys play dominoes, although calling them *boys* wasn't exactly accurate. Joe was the oldest out of the four, but there didn't seem to be a lot in it. The other three were chatting away but as soon as they saw Chris, they stopped. One by one they got to their feet and shook hands with him. Not one of them mentioned his dad but they all gave him a pat on the back, wished him a happy birthday and invited him to join the game. Chris had never played dominoes in his life and declined. He was happy just to watch and join in with the conversation.

The snug was exactly that – snug. It was wide enough for a table to seat four, six at a push, with a small fireplace at one end. If the fire was ever used, the snug would become an oven.

Unsurprisingly given Joe's nature, the game was extremely competitive and loose change seemed to be passing rapidly from one side of the table to the other. In between grumpy exchanges, the men talked about anything and everything. Although Chris had never met any of the men before, they were familiar with Ollie and Lou. When they asked about Ollie learning to ride his bike and how his new school was suiting him, he smiled and looked at Joe. Joe didn't look back, he was too busy scrutinising his tiles, but Chris knew Joe probably talked to these men about little else other than his great-grandson.

An hour passed pleasantly. It was clear the men knew each other for most of their lives. They had raised their own families and in turn had seen their sons and daughters raise their own families. It was normal life but none had experienced what Joe had gone through. Thank God, none of them had gone through that.

"Here they are!" Pat Bailey stood in the doorway to the snug, or rather he leaned on the doorframe. None of the men looked up but there were several sighs.

Joe was the only one to speak.

"Evening, lad. Are you having a game?"

"Not me, Joe. You boys'd bleed me dry." He lifted his head. "Chris, you buying me a drink then?"

Pat's slur was evident for everyone to hear and it sounded

like his volume dial was broken.

Chris stood up and sidled past the chairs to the door. "Come on then." He guided Pat out of the snug and back to the bar. He had a feeling this was a regular occurrence and not a particularly welcome one for the domino players.

"Two Rattlers please, Susie, and he's paying," Pat shouted although Susie was standing right in front of him.

Chris looked at the barmaid. "I'll just have half a Tribute, please."

"What? What's the matter with you?" Pat banged his fist on the bar. "He's not like his old man, is he?" He looked at Susie who just looked back at him without offering an opinion.

"I'm driving, Pat. I've got to get the old boy home, haven't I?" He hoped his answer would soften the undercurrent of hostility in Pat's demeanour.

"Ah, you won't find a bloody copper around here at this time. They're all over in Penzance with their feet up."

"Just half." Chris smiled at Susie. "And a Rattler for Pat, cheers."

"Suit yourself." Pat clapped him on the back and drained the last half of his current pint in one go.

"So how's about you and me take a drive later?"

Chris paid Susie. He didn't want any more to drink but he took a sip to placate Pat. "A drive? Where to?"

Pat took his cider and started pouring it down his throat. He didn't seem to swallow and when he stopped, half of it was gone.

"I thought I could show you all the places your dad and

me used to go." He turned and winked at Susie.

"I don't know. I need to drive Granddad back home and…"

"Come on, it'll be Bailey and Kestle back on the road again. I've got some new ones?" He winked at Chris now.

The thought of being in a car with a drunk wasn't attractive, even if it was his dad's best friend. But the idea of hearing something new about his dad had a certain appeal to it. It wasn't a good idea, not with Pat like this, but still…

"I'll come back and pick you up after I've dropped him off. Just don't go too heavy on that, okay?" He pointed at the glass in Pat's hand.

Pat put the glass down on the bar and offered his hand. "Scout's honour."

Chris shook it and put a five pound note on the bar. "That's for the last one." He walked back to the snug and sat down.

"Everything okay?" Joe asked without looking up.

"He's just having his last one."

One of the other men grunted. "He's getting to be a real pain in the arse is Pat."

It was noticeable that none of the others disagreed.

"That he is," said Joe flatly.

Chapter 9

Chris pulled the car in but didn't turn off the engine.

"Are you planning on sitting out here all night?" Joe had his hand on the door handle.

"I'm going back to see Pat. He wants to take a drive and see the places him and Dad used to go to." He stopped and looked at Joe. "I don't know if it's catharsis for him but he looks like he needs something."

"Just be careful. I love him like my own but he isn't right. He isn't the man your dad grew up with."

"It's the booze. I've only been here a couple of days and both times I've seen him he's been…"

"Yes," Joe interrupted, "and he's been like that for a while now, so you just be careful." Joe climbed out of the car and tapped the roof with his hand.

Chris watched him go inside and put the car into reverse. He had an idea that this was catharsis for both him and Pat. He'd heard Pat's stories, some of them several times, and he'd been to most of the places in those stories but never put the two together. He hoped they would add up to more than the sum of their parts when they were joined.

He drove into the village. He could see a dark shape sitting on the steps to the war memorial. His mind went back to the morning and the shadow on the cemetery shed. The headlights swooped around and lit up the hunched figure. His head was down but there was no mistaking Pat. He looked like he was having a snooze, but as soon as Chris pulled up alongside, he jerked into life. Chris noticed the four-pack in his hand.

"Supplies," he announced as climbed inside.

"I thought I said no more." Chris felt his heart sink and turned the engine off. He didn't need the night to turn into a bickering match with a bad-tempered drunk. Nor did he want to sound like a babysitter.

"I didn't have any more. I thought we'd have a toast to Jack later."

Chris scrutinised him. Pat looked sincere, although judging by the state of his speech he'd had some more, plenty more.

"Okay but just one."

Pat chuckled. "Of course. Just one."

Chris started the engine again. "Okay, so where to first?"

"Oh, it's got to be the park."

"You mean, Cape Park? Just over there?" Chris pointed up the road. The park was on the road out toward the cemetery, but not as far.

Pat nodded. "Go on, I'll tell you a story about your dad

and some dark deeds in the park." He grinned like a maniac.

Chris shook his head and started driving. He'd taken Ollie in the park when he was a toddler. The swings and the slide were marked by rust, and the football pitch had been overgrown and unused. It was dismal in the day. As he pulled into the car park, he realised it was equally so at night.

As soon as the car stopped, Pat opened the first can of cider. Chris took one too but he had no intention of drinking more than a mouthful.

"Switch the lights on."

Chris did as he was asked.

"In there," Pat started and pointed at the trees around the football pitch, "is where your dad took Susie Curnow's bra off and squeezed her tits. We were fourteen and it was your dad's maiden voyage. He didn't stop smiling for a whole week."

Chris thought back to the pub. "Not the same Susie from The Queen's?"

Pat laughed and held his can up to the window. "The very same. Mind you, she soon wiped the smile off his face when she found out he'd been telling half the school about it. To Jack!" He took a drink and Chris did the same.

Was this something he needed to know? He smiled. Of course it was. "Where next then?"

"Trewellard Arms," Pat said without hesitation and took Chris's can off him.

It was a ten minute drive to the next destination but Pat didn't stop talking all the way there. The stories were just minor incidents at school resulting on one or both of them getting into trouble, but Pat spoke about them as if they were just yesterday, and was very animated.

Closing time had long passed and The Trewellard Arms was in darkness when Chris drove into the car park. It was a place he'd never been in but had often passed on the way to St Ives.

"This, my boy, was the first pub your dad ever bought me a drink."

Chris nodded.

"This was back in the Sixties and it was my fifteenth birthday. We caught the bus up here 'cos we knew we wouldn't have a hope of getting served at The Queen's." He paused and smiled as if he were picturing it. "Jack walks straight up to the bar, bold as brass, and leans on it with an Embassy hanging from the corner of his mouth. 'Two pints of cider please, love,' he says. He didn't look more than ten years old and she took one look at him and said 'You ain't old enough.' He just looked at her and put the money on the bar. 'Two pints of cider, please.' Well, she just tutted and poured our drinks. Everyone used to say he was the shy one out of the two of us, but he weren't, not when you got to know him. He had more bottle than half of the school. We had four pints each that night and we were both as sick as dogs."

Pat threw his head back and laughed. "Joe had him up at five pulling them pots and he was throwing up the whole trip. Joe didn't give a rat's arse about him puking up like that, just told him to get on with it, but Jack never did that to Joe again."

Chris laughed too. Joe wouldn't have cared if he'd been half-dead. Pulling the lobster pots was all that mattered.

"What about you, did your dad give you a roasting?"

Pat's face changed. "My old man was probably asleep in the gutter, covered in his own piss and too drunk to know where his bed was." He passed a can back to Chris. "Here's to Jack." He took a long drink and crumpled his can before dropping it into the footwell.

They both sat in silence for a minute. Pat opened his second can and took several long swallows from it.

"How about the lighthouse?" Chris suggested. "Pendeen's just down the road." He knew his dad and Pat had been there on numerous occasions, especially once they had access to a car. He reversed out of the car park without waiting for a reply. Pat was just staring out of the side window in silence. Chris knew Joe had helped raise Pat in the absence of his own father and thinking about the man obviously had a bad effect on him. He was morose, but once they got to the lighthouse he would start up again.

It was a couple of minutes before he spoke.

"I don't want to go there."

Chris pulled onto the access road and switched the main beam on. It was pitch black and he knew the track was full of crater-like potholes. It was wide enough for only one car and wound down toward the coast. It wouldn't do the car any good but they were nearly there now.

"What? We're more or less there." The flashing beacon from the lighthouse was brilliant in the darkness.

"I said, I don't want to go there. I want to go home now."

Pat had been happy up until that point but the mixture of alcohol and a mention of his dad had changed things in his head.

"Pat, I can't turn round and I'm not reversing all the way back up there, so there's not much I can do about it now."

Pat remained silent.

There wasn't a car park next to the lighthouse, just a worn patch of grass that people used. Chris pulled onto it and turned the ignition. Pat was still staring out of the window and hadn't said a word for some time. Whatever was going on in his head, he was keeping to himself.

He opened the door and the sound of the ocean filled the car. "I'm going for a whizz, Pat, back in a minute."

"We used to bring girls up here." Pat carried on staring out of the window. "When we had the car, that was."

Chris stopped but left the door open. It was chilly but it would be a crime to shut the door on the cool smell of sea spray.

"We'd bring a carry-out from the pub and go sit down there." He tapped his finger on the window glass. "We'd dare each other to see who could get closest to the edge. The more we drank, the closer we got." He turned to Chris. "Pretty stupid, eh?"

Chris shrugged and they were both silent again. Doing stupid things was pretty much a prerequisite of growing up, especially where boys were concerned.

"So how come you've never met anyone, Pat?" He regretted the question immediately. It was tactless.

Pat grunted. "I've been lucky, haven't I?" He paused and

turned his head away from the window for the first time in ten minutes. "Maybe I did and maybe things didn't work out. For either of us." He took a long drink and released a loud belch.

That was about as philosophical as he'd ever heard Pat get.

"Still time. You just need to give that a rest." He flicked the can Pat had in his hand.

Pat burped again and licked his lips. That was his response to Chris's remark.

Chris climbed out of the car. "Right, I'm going for that walk. Coming?"

Pat opened the last can. "Nope."

Chris dropped down the bank using the whitewashed perimeter wall to guide him. He could hear the waves crashing into the rocks below and although he knew it was some distance to the cliff edge, he was still nervous because it was so dark. There was no access to the lighthouse and part of the building had been turned into holiday cottages. There were no lights from inside the complex except for the huge lighthouse itself.

He looked up at the lantern. He remembered coming here with his dad and doing the same thing. He counted in his head and just before he reached four, the bulb winked, sending its warning beacon out onto the black mass of sea. It was a beautiful place, night or day.

He unzipped, closed his eyes and listened to the waves. He was getting better by the day. By the time Ollie and Lou came, he'd be back to how he was before all of this. He might even be able to write something…

He opened his eyes immediately. A sound had pushed the waves aside. A man-made sound. It was the engine on his car revving loudly.

He zipped up and started walking back up the slope. "Come on, Pat," he whispered.

When he got to the top, he stopped. Partly because he was a little out of breath but mostly because of what he could see. The Volvo wasn't where he'd parked it. Pat had managed to move it and the front wheels were on the slope. The car was pointing at him, at the cliff, and the engine was revving with a constant high-pitched whine.

"Pat!" he shouted as loudly as he could but he knew there was no way Pat could hear him. He started running until his legs went from under him. It wasn't exertion this time, it was something else entirely. It was terror.

The car was lit momentarily by the lighthouse and then was dark again. But in that brief moment, he saw a twisted black shadow on the bonnet and a look of absolute horror burned onto Pat's face.

Pat was in the driver's seat and his foot was obviously jammed down on the gas and the brake. If he took his foot off the brake, the car would hurtle down the slope and kill them both.

He had to move, he had to do something, but what he'd seen on the car was what he'd seen at the cemetery. He closed his eyes, counted to three then opened them.

The shadow crept up the windscreen, and as the light went out again, Chris knew the shape was human; twisted and deformed, but human. The car lurched forward. Even above the screech of the engine, he heard the sound of Pat's scream. It was a horrible sound. The pitch was wrong for Pat, all wrong.

"Move, move, move!" he shouted and scrambled to his feet. He counted in his head for the next strobe from the lantern but he was still ten metres away from the car and his legs felt like jelly.

"Pat," he shouted, "get off the gas!" It was hopeless but he did it anyway.

And then the beam hit the car again and the light seemed to last an eternity. Pat's hands were covering his eyes, his mouth ajar in a silent scream.

She – and Chris knew it was a she now – turned and swept toward him like a cloak billowing in a storm. He'd seen that face before. He'd seen it in his nightmares, in his daydreams, and at Hawk's Cove on that day. And now she was here, right in front of him again. He staggered back, the sound of the waves and the engine forgotten and lost.

"I can see you," she hissed.

There were no eyes, there had never been any eyes, just empty voids. In those deep and dark pits was a feeling of hopelessness, of desperation and of hatred. Of hell.

He fell back again. The cliff edge was behind him, he knew it was, and yet he couldn't stop himself. She *could* see him. She knew what was down there, buried deep in his soul. It was the same thing that was in his dad's soul. It was the same thing that had made him put pen to paper and write that note.

He needed to keep walking. He needed to go over that precipice. Down there, on the blackened and jagged rocks was the answer to everything. Ollie would under…

"Ollie?" His own voice startled him. This wasn't right, this wasn't how it was supposed to be for him, for Ollie or for Lou. He hadn't come here for this.

He had stopped staggering backwards but his eyes were still fixed on her. He knew that if she pushed again, he would be powerless to resist.

The lighthouse foghorn blasted into the air. The depth of its tone sent what felt like a shockwave flying at him, he could feel his flesh rippling under its impact. He staggered again but now he could hear another sound.

The horn on the car was sounding frantically in time with the beat of his heart. There were lights too. Pat was switching them on and off rapidly and revving the engine to breaking point, creating a piercing, whining sound.

He looked away from her to the car. Whatever spell she had cast was broken.

"I can see you there, Chris."

Her words were a faint whisper on the wind and then she was gone. She was gone.

He crawled back up the slope toward the car, all the time praying that Pat would keep his size twelves firmly on the brake. The car was still revving and in the lighthouse beam he could see Pat banging on the centre of the steering wheel, sounding the horn.

"Keep hitting it, Pat. Just keep banging it," he muttered as he crept closer. The sound was like a beacon for him. A sign that he was getting closer to safety and proof that he was still alive.

He reached the car and touched the bumper. He could feel the heat coming from the engine. It was a good car but if Pat carried on much longer, it would blow up.

He clambered to his feet and yelled, "Enough!" Pat's face, momentarily illuminated, was almost the most terrible thing he'd seen all night. Almost, but not quite.

He ran to the driver's side and opened the door. "Handbrake on and move over."

Pat stared back at him. His mouth was wide open.

"Pat, put the fucking handbrake on and move!"

Pat reached down and pulled the brake without pressing the button. The ratcheting sound was reassuring. Chris started clambering in before Pat had fully moved but he couldn't wait any longer.

He barely registered how hot the steering wheel was as he pushed the car into reverse and released the handbrake. The front wheels tried to gain purchase but the car didn't move an inch. He looked over his shoulder into the darkness. It was a better option than looking down the hill. He eased down on the gas harder. He hoped to God he wouldn't have to get out again. He prayed he wouldn't have to push the car up the hill. Pat didn't seem capable of doing anything except staring, and his own legs felt like they were made of rubber.

"Come on," he hissed through gritted teeth. "Move."

He pressed down even harder. He was conscious the car would dig a rut in the earth and become stuck but he needed the extra gas to move. He felt the front of the car start to slip to the side, jammed the pedal down to the floor as hard as he could.

The car lurched violently. As soon as he felt it start to level out, he cranked the steering wheel around to full lock. He didn't care if there was a stone wall behind the car. He didn't even care if the engine was completely shot. It just had to last long enough to get them out of there. He pounded over the potholes without trying to avoid them this time. If there was anything coming the other way, well they better just get into the hedge because he was coming through, one way or another.

He didn't take his foot off the gas until they reached The Trewellard Arms and he skidded into the car park like an eighteen year old boy racer. If there had been any other cars parked up he would have hit them all, each and every one.

He collapsed against the steering wheel, resting his head on the hot and sweaty leather. His breaths came in ragged spurts. It was as if he'd sprinted the last couple of miles while holding his breath, not driven them.

"Pat? You okay?" He didn't look up. He couldn't just yet but there was no reply. The car smelled of body odour, the sour stench of an alcoholic's pores opening up, and spilled cider.

"Pat?"

"Yes, yes… yes I'm okay."

He sounded far from okay but at least it was some form of response. Chris could feel his body shiver and shake now, and the feeling in his stomach told him there was a good chance he might vomit. He opened the window a crack and took several deep breaths. The streetlights cast an orange glow over the car and he was grateful for it. The light was constant. It didn't flash every four seconds, it didn't show things that weren't supposed to be there. It was normal.

"What... was... that?" he asked. His head was still pressed into the steering wheel. "What *was* it?"

He heard Pat exhale loudly but said nothing. He just shifted in his seat.

Chris straightened and looked at him. "Pat, what was it?" Even under the warming orange glow of the lights, the man looked pale. A dark patch covered his chest. It was either sweat, cider or a horrible mixture of the two.

"Nothing," he replied.

"What?" Had he heard him right? "What did you say?" He shifted in his seat so he could see Pat better.

"I said, it was nothing." Pat looked straight ahead. "I'd like to go back now."

Chris couldn't say a word. He'd seen Pat's eyes. He'd seen the look of absolute terror scratched across his face and now he was sitting there as if nothing had happened. He wasn't mad. Pat had looked into the eyes of that thing, just like he had.

"You saw it! You saw the same thing I saw!"

"I'd like you to drive back to the village and drop..."

"Look at me. Look at me, Pat." He could hear the anger in his voice and it scared him.

Pat didn't move a muscle, he just sat there. Chris could feel desperation joining the anger. Both were close to the surface.

Chris grabbed his shoulder. Pat was bloated but the years of pulling lobster pots hadn't melted away his muscles yet.

"Please, Pat. Just turn and face me and tell me you didn't see her."

Pat turned slowly and looked at him. He was ill and it wasn't the streetlights that made him look that way. They just amplified what was already there. He opened his mouth to speak and left it hanging for a moment. "I don't know what you want me say."

"You looked into her eyes, same as I did. The same holes I looked into at Hawk's when... when Dad died. You saw her, Pat, you saw her."

Pat wiped a hand across his beard. "I saw nothing. She wasn't there, Chris. Not then and not now. You made her..."

Chris didn't wait for him to finish his sentence, he knew what was coming. He swung his fist and hit Pat in the cheek. There wasn't much force in the blow, he hadn't got the leverage, but Pat's head snapped to the side.

"You bastard!" he yelled and swung his fist again. This time Pat lifted his shoulder, deflected the blow and shoved him with two meaty hands. It sent Chris into his door, the electric window control panel jammed painfully into his back.

"You saw nothing," Pat said with his teeth bared. "Nothing at all."

Chris hadn't punched anyone since a fight at school and his hand throbbed already. The punch hadn't been thrown out of anger but out of frustration and desperation, and now he regretted it. Pat was his dad's oldest friend. He would no more want to hurt the man that he would Joe.

"Pat, I'm sorry. It was…"

Pat banged his fist on the dashboard. "Not another word, Chris. Not another word. Just drive us back."

Chris stared at him. "You've seen her before, haven't you?" There was no way any sane person could see what they had both just seen and pretend it hadn't happened. Not unless you had seen it before.

"Please, I'm asking you to take me home." Pat's voice was firm and emotionless.

Chris started the engine. He would take Pat home but this conversation wasn't finished. Not by a long way.

*

Chris pulled over at the memorial. "Sure you want to get out here?"

"I need some fresh air." Pat turned in his seat. "Your old man had a lousy right hook too. He couldn't fight his way out of a paper bag." He opened the door. "I'll show you how to throw a proper punch tomorrow. You need to be able to show that lad of yours how to defend himself."

He laughed and climbed out. It was as if nothing had happened. Chris wished with all his soul that nothing had happened; not the pathetic punch, not any of it.

He watched Pat walk across the square. The country was littered with men just like him; men who had, for one reason or another, allowed life to beat them up. He looked a sad figure as he shambled his way past the darkened shops and up the hill. The dark patch covering his crotch and thighs confirmed what Chris already knew. Pat had seen her and she had literally scared the piss out of him.

"Go home, Pat, and we'll talk about this tomorrow," he whispered and drove away.

He'd already decided what tomorrow would bring. There would be a long conversation with Pat at his house and he wouldn't be brushed away quite so easily.

He drove down the winding lane toward Joe's cottage. His heartbeat had slowed since Pendeen but it was still echoing in his ears. It would probably be like that until tomorrow. He wound down the window to let in some fresh air. The nutty smell of autumn hadn't fully hit yet, the gorse still had its sweet coconut scent to offer and it slipped into the car.

The high stone walls, covered in gorse, moss and bramble, loomed over the car as they always did. Although it was impossible, tonight they felt aggressive and challenging as if they didn't really want him there. It was a claustrophobic couple of miles and he was relieved to see the beam of light from Joe's kitchen shining onto the road. It was the finish line for tonight.

Beyond it, beyond the welcoming light of the cottage, was the road to Hawk's Cove and that was where he needed to go. That was ultimately where he had to go. First though, he needed a drink.

Joe never locked the door. Chris walked straight in and opened the cupboard where he knew the Bushmills was kept. It was definitely a night for some Irish but without the coffee. He poured a good measure, swallowed it in one then poured himself another. He pulled a chair out and sat down with both the glass and the bottle in front of him. It wasn't possible what had happened at Pendeen. On no level was that possible. It wasn't possible what he'd seen in Ollie's sketch or to have seen *her* standing behind Ollie at the party either. And what he'd seen in the sitting room picture was inconceivable. Yet it had all happened.

If Pat hadn't been there tonight, he would have assumed he was mad; that he had gone even lower than either he or Lou had thought. But Pat *had* been there and he *had* seen it. Pat was a drunk, but two people seeing the same thing wasn't down to alcohol, especially when one of them had only taken a couple of sips. And then there was his reaction. The shock and fear had dissipated so quickly. There was no fuss and he'd refused to comment. Why, why, why?

He drained the second tumbler and poured another. He could feel the warmth spreading through his body but his brain wasn't connected to the whiskey yet. What would have happened if he'd just kept walking backwards away from her, away from her eyes? He'd have ended up in a bloody, mangled bag of bones like his dad. But it had been easy to give in, to just look into those voids and see the desperation, the loss of hope and of utter contempt, and give in to it. Is that what he'd glimpsed from her on the slipway at Hawk's Cove? If there had been a foghorn then, perhaps none of it would have happened.

He drank half of the measure and put the glass down. He didn't remember there being any fog but he hadn't really been on the lookout for it. The sound of the foghorn was a bleak one, almost as desolate as her eyes. It made a horrible backdrop for her voice in his head.

"One more ought to do it." He topped up the glass and downed it in one. It bit his throat on the way down but the brief exposure to the fresh air and the previous doses had given him what he was looking for – a spinning and insensible mind.

He tried the door handle again to make sure it was locked and turned off the light. There were shadows everywhere. Familiar shapes in the darkness, some he didn't recognise and he'd have to walk past them to get to the stairs. He paused for a moment and switched the light back on. He was being childish, he knew he was, he was acting like Ollie did when he had a nightmare. It was irrational to someone looking in from the outside, but to him it was as real as… as real as what he'd seen at Pendeen.

He walked across the kitchen and took the dark stairs as quickly as he could without making too much noise and waking Joe. The whiskey had seemed like a good idea but now he wasn't quite so sure. It had nullified the sensible part of his brain and fed the other half. The half which had her inside. The half with a voice which said, 'I can see you,' over and over and over again against the backdrop of the Pendeen foghorn.

He switched the lamp on and collapsed onto the bed. The voice was relentless and spiteful. It was deafening. He clamped his hands over his ears but it wasn't coming from outside, it was coming from inside and there would be no quietening of it. Not tonight, not ever.

Chapter 10

"I wish you'd spoken to me first. Ollie was full of it last night." Lou sounded tense.

"I thought it might help." Chris hadn't slept very well and he felt strained too. "He said he didn't want to go to bed. I just thought if he was thinking about coming here it would distract him. I did try to talk to you but you were…"

"Oh yeah, that worked until about three o'clock this morning and then it was bad, really bad."

"Nightmares?" It was a stupid question.

"Screaming, thrashing. He was hysterical, I didn't know what to do with him."

"That's it, I'm coming home."

"And do what, Chris? What exactly will you do when you get here? Frighten him some more when you see *her*? Scare him when you think you've seen a ghost in one of his pictures? What will you do? You tell me?" She wasn't just tense, she was angry.

"I just…"

"You're no use to us at the moment. You'll do more harm than good."

The words stung but she was right. Especially how he felt after last night. "But I'm feeling better, that's why I suggested half-term. I'll be fine by then, I promise. I'm getting there, I promise you, I'm getting there."

There was silence from the other end.

"Is he there? Can I speak to him?"

"He's in the shower, he wet the bed again. Talk to him tonight, okay?" Her tone had softened.

"I can hang on?"

"Tonight, Chris. Speak to him tonight."

There wasn't much he could do. "He'll get over the nightmares. It's just a bad phase."

He heard Lou grunt. This was as close to agreement as he was going to get.

"He thinks there's someone in his room, that's why he won't go to bed."

"Someone in his room? Who does he think it is?"

"I don't know and he won't talk about it. I don't want to push him about it either, it'll just make things worse, so don't mention it when you talk to him later. Okay?"

"Okay, if you think that's best." He wasn't sure but Lou was the one dealing with it, not him.

"Talk to you later then."

"Half-term? Ollie would love it, and so would Joe."

"I'll be speaking to Joe before we go anywhere. I need to make sure, Chris. You understand that, don't you?"

"Of course I do." They ended the call. It finished with them on better terms than they had been at the beginning but it was a long way from happy families.

Chris was still lying on top of the bed, where he'd collapsed. He was still dressed in the same clothes as he'd worn last night and they smelled of body odour and cider. He stripped off, changed and bundled his clothes up to go in the washing machine. He had no idea what time Pat woke up or what time his daily drinking ritual began, but he wanted to be there early.

At some point he'd fallen asleep, he must have done because his alarm woke him up, but he couldn't remember at which point his eyes had grown too heavy to keep open. He'd stared at the ceiling for so long that he could almost see her shape forming in the darkness. At one point the sound of her voice had been broken by another sound, the sound of screaming. But it had been a dream, a thin and nasty dream, inhabiting the space just under the lightest levels of sleep, where every sound was as real as if it were in the room with him.

He was pushing the clothes into the machine when Joe came in.

"It's a chilly one." Joe rubbed his hands together and walked straight over to the kettle. "It's blowing a gale out there. I wouldn't be going out fishing today. Tea?"

"Please, I was just about to make one but these are a bit ripe."

"Yep, a night out with Pat will do that." He pointed to the Bushmills bottle and the glass on the table. "And it'll do that to you too."

Chris stood up and winced. The bottle was now almost empty. "Sorry, I'll get some more today."

"Don't worry. How was he?" Joe was already boiling a pan of water for the eggs.

"Drunk. At least I think he was. It's hard to tell with him at the moment."

"No change there then. Where did he take you?"

Chris was trying hard not to think about it. Not yet, not until he'd spoken to Pat again.

"We drove up the road to the park, up along the road to St Ives to The Trewellard. Just a general drive about really." He deliberately left out the visit to Pendeen and to the lighthouse.

Joe turned and smiled. "Told you some stories about your dad, did he?"

Chris smiled back but he didn't much feel like it. "He did. A couple you might not have heard before."

Joe turned back to the pan and put two slices of bread into the toaster. "And if Pat was involved then I probably don't want to hear them either."

Chris took the tumbler from the table and rinsed it.

"You needed the drink to settle you back down, I imagine. A night with Pat can be hard work."

Chris put the bottle back in the cupboard. "Something like that, Granddad."

*

Chris drove up the lane toward the village. He had left Joe listening to the shipping forecast on Radio Four. It wasn't particularly important for Joe to hear it anymore but after so many years, it was a habit he refused to break. The windscreen wipers activated automatically as a light but steady drizzle fell. It was just after half past eight which he had a feeling was early for Pat, but he didn't care. The longer he sat with Joe trying not to think about Pendeen, the more it crept into his thoughts. The more *she* crept into his thoughts.

Pat lived in a terraced house on a street, tucked back on the way out of the village. The houses had all belonged to miners when the industry was thriving but there were no miners there now. The street was a dead end and at the bottom there was a Methodist chapel. Someone with a lot of money had bought it several years ago and turned it into a place where glossy magazines went to photograph the latest interior designs. The exterior wasn't pretty but it was dominant.

He pulled up outside Pat's. The downstairs curtains were open which was a good sign but it wasn't conclusive. Pat was the sort of man who went to bed without bothering about whether curtains were drawn or not. Chris had brought Ollie here once as a baby but never brought him back. Back then Pat hadn't been anywhere near as bad with the booze, but even then keeping a clean house had been low on his list of priorities.

He got out of the car and banged on the door. He was determined this was not going to degenerate into another row or even a fight. He wasn't under the same pressure as he'd been last night. Neither of them were. In the cold light of day, there was no way Pat could deny any of it.

He banged again and stepped back into the road. The upstairs curtains were open too. He cupped his hands around his face and peered in through the downstairs window. The window was foggy, not through the weather but from the build-up of grease and grime. It was just as he remembered. There was a small sofa, a coffee table in front of a ragged-looking armchair, and a television. There was a kitchen beyond that but the window was too dirty to see much detail that far back in the house. It didn't go unnoticed that there was a number of cider cans and an empty two-litre bottle on the table. If that was breakfast, then he was setting himself up for a good day.

He pushed the letterbox open and shouted, "Pat, it's Chris. You in there?" The air inside smelled stale. "Pat?"

He allowed the letterbox to close and stepped back into the road again. He could be ignoring him of course, but that wouldn't be like Pat. He was argumentative, belligerent and occasionally aggressive but never ignorant.

Where to now then? Pat didn't have a car anymore. That had gone around the same time as his licence had been taken off him by the court, so he never went very far. Chris looked up and down the street and bit his lip. He needed to get some more Bushmills for Joe and some other supplies to make them both dinner tonight. He was going to make him a chilli, hopefully one with enough *poke* to satisfy the old boy.

There was Pat to think about though. He really needed to speak to him. He banged on the window one last time and climbed back into the car. If he couldn't find him now, he knew where he would be come eleven o'clock – in The Queen's. It wasn't ideal but it might do for a start.

He drove back into the village and parked up on the square. It was virtually empty except for a few faces he vaguely recognised. He sat for a few minutes hoping Pat might spring from one of the shops, from the butcher's or the bakery, but he never did.

The Co-op was similarly quiet which was good because the shop was tiny; in the summer months, customers queued all the way around the store. He chose what he needed and walked to the till.

"Hello again." A voice came from behind.

He turned and saw it was the barmaid from the pub, Susie Curnow. The image of the park flashed through his mind. The park where his dad had removed her bra.

"Hi, how's it going?" he asked.

"Not too bad, yourself?"

He paid the young lad at the till and took his bags away. "Good thanks," he lied. "You haven't seen Pat this morning, have you?"

Susie blew air loudly through her pursed lips. "I see him every day and not once has it been before opening time."

Chris nodded and started to walk away. "Okay, cheers. Have a good one."

"He wasn't a bad-looking lad when he was younger." She followed him out. "Not as handsome as your dad, mind, but he was…" She sighed loudly. "Now look at him. He needs a good woman to sort him out."

They walked together for a few strides until Chris reached the car. He opened it and put the bags on the back seat. "Can I give you a lift anywhere, Susie?"

She opened her mouth but whatever she said was immediately swallowed up by the sound of a siren screaming toward them. First a police car raced past then an ambulance quickly followed behind.

Both vehicles turned onto the road leading to Joe's cottage and Hawk's Cove.

Chris jumped into the car without saying another word and drove away. His tyres squealed on the road as his foot pressed hard on the accelerator. The car had taken a battering over the last few hours and it was about to be tested again. His heart sank as he drove down the lane. There was only a handful of cottages on the road and if it was Joe… he couldn't bear to allow his thoughts to go any further down that line.

Another siren blared from behind. He looked in the mirror and saw flashing headlights and a pulsing blue beacon bright in the mirror. It was almost on top of him but there weren't many passing places on the road. He drove as quickly as he could and the driver, seeing there was nowhere to pass, switched off both the sirens and the lights.

As soon as he was able, Chris pulled over and let the police car pass. He immediately pressed down on the pedal and tried to keep up with it. As he rounded the final bend, he expected to see a collection of liveried emergency vehicles lined up outside Joe's cottage. It was then that he released his breath. He had no idea how long he'd been holding it for but it erupted from his mouth with a bellow. There were no more houses farther down the lane, so unless there had been an accident on the road, there was only one place the ambulance and police cars were going.

He slowed the car down outside Joe's but didn't pull in. He wasn't about to go gawking at some unfortunate person's accident, especially when it was at Hawk's Cove, but something about this didn't feel right.

"Go on!"

He'd been staring so intently down the lane that he hadn't seen Joe come out of the cottage. He was climbing into the passenger seat.

"I don't like the feel of this, lad. Not at all." Joe grimaced as he sat down.

Chris pushed down on the accelerator and they moved away. This was the first time he'd passed the invisible line he'd scratched into the road since his dad had died. There was a sign too, a sign that only he could see and on that sign it said 'DO NOT PASS!" in bright red letters. He glanced at it as he drove past. The letters were running down the sign and dripping onto the grass like blood.

"Nor do I." He looked at the road ahead, watching the blue beacons swinging one way then the other as the drivers navigated the lane.

As soon as he turned around the first corner, nausea hit him like a freight train. It rose quickly up from his guts and coated his mouth in sour bile. He swallowed it back and wound the window down.

"You okay, boy?"

Chris nodded once and swung the car around the bend. The view that opened up took his breath away and at the same time sent a ripple of nausea up his throat. He heaved and spat the acid out of the window.

"It's beautiful," he whispered. And it was, it was one of the most dazzling vistas he could imagine. It was also hideous.

"They're all down there." Joe pointed toward the car park. It was unnecessary because that was where the road ended. There was nothing more except for a path down to the cove. He knew it well. As much as he tried to scrub it from his mind, it was all imprinted on his memory in high-resolution clarity. He drove forward slowly and parked near the top, out of the way of the emergency vehicles.

He knew every inch of Hawk's Cove as if he'd lived in it for the last thirty-three years. In a way he had. Joe started to climb out of the car. "You stay there."

Joe's face was lined with battle scars. They were deep and would never heal. Battling to keep going – to stay alive when God had kicked him in the nuts, not once but twice – had made his face a patchwork of pain. He covered it up with a smile and a wink but it was still there and you didn't need to look very hard to see it.

Chris sat there for a moment and watched him walk down the gradient toward the ambulance. Joe's slight figure disappeared for a split-second as the wipers flashed across the screen. He turned the engine off and opened the door. The air smelled different here. The sea spray was like glitter, lacing the air with a tangy metallic odour that filled his head with fear.

"No!" It was Joe's voice, there was no mistaking it. He followed it up by smashing his fist against the side of the ambulance. It was louder than the sound of the waves raking the pebbles below.

"No, no, no!" He looked up at Chris and put his hands to his head. "No!" he roared and fell against the side of the ambulance.

Chris waited. To move would be to take a step closer to the cove, to his own hell. To simply wait would be to leave Joe in agony. He'd been too young and too locked in his grief to see what Joe had gone through when his dad had died. And nobody except Joe knew what losing Lizzy had done to him. But as Chris looked at him through the steady fall of rain, he knew it would take something like that to reduce him to this. No, not something *like* that. *Exactly* that.

To stay where he was wasn't an option. To leave the man he loved as a father, crumpled against the side of an ambulance like that, was unthinkable. He sprinted down the incline and took Joe in his arms.

"He said he was going to do it one day. He told me what he was going to do," Joe wailed.

He was sobbing and his body was heaving but as Chris held him, he looked over his shoulder into the cove. Everything was there, just as he remembered it, down to each tiny, insignificant detail; the colour of the pebbles, the tangle of lobster pots, the fishing boats and the dazzling whiteness of the ocean smashing into the rocks. Everything was there but this time there was something else. There was someone else, somebody who hadn't been there last time.

There was a body. A body which leaked blood as black as the ocean from two deep ravines cut into his wrists. Pat Bailey's body lay as if he'd been crucified.

Chapter 11

The blood was congealing in two long streaks down the slipway. It looked thick and black like an oil spill from one of the fishing boats. The tide was coming in and the waves tasted the ends of the blood trails before coming back and nibbling at them again. The sea had always enjoyed the taste of human blood. Always.

There was no mistaking Pat. His unkempt beard and grubby, green and red chequered shirt were all anyone would need to identify him. There were two policemen and two paramedics down there with him. Their fluorescent coats were a dazzling contrast to both the bleak backdrop and the awful situation. They gathered around him as if there was something that could be done to help him, to save him.

One of the paramedics looked up at them and said something to his colleague before walking up the path toward the car park. Joe had stopped sobbing but he clung to Chris as Chris had clung to him many times before.

Chris looked down on the scene and hoped someone else, *something else*, wouldn't decide to make an appearance. But all of the time, the sea raked the pebbles and hissed at him in a warning. *Keep back.*

The paramedic approached them. "Do you know him?" he asked quietly, out of breath. His hair was plastered to his head with rain.

"I do," Chris replied. "We both do."

"I'm sorry." He opened the back of the ambulance and pulled out a collapsible trolley.

"We're going to bring him up now. The police will want to speak to you."

"His name is Pat." Joe pushed Chris gently away and stood up straight. "Patrick Bailey."

The paramedic nodded and smiled. "Well, we're going to bring Patrick back up here as gently and as quickly as we can. Okay?"

Joe just stared without saying a word as the paramedic wheeled the trolley down the path. Chris watched him as he went. "Why Pat, why?" He didn't love Pat the way his dad had or the way Joe did but there was a bond between them, between them all.

Joe rummaged in his pocket and pushed a piece of paper at Chris, who read it aloud. "I'm sorry, I'm sorry, I'm sorry." The paper was covered in the same words over and over again. He looked back at Joe. "Is this from him?"

Joe nodded. "It was on the mat this morning."

"What? Why didn't you say anything?"

"Because I've got a drawer full of them back at home. I've

lost count of how many there are." Joe's voice started to break but he fought to control it. "He hasn't got anyone else. Just me and I couldn't help him either." He looked up at Chris. "I can't help anyone, can I?"

Chris put his hand on Joe's cheek. "Don't, Granddad. There's me, you've always helped me."

Joe wiped his face. It might have been the rain or it might have been tears, there was no way of knowing. "The jury's still out on that one."

They turned away from each other and watched in silence as Pat was lifted onto the trolley. The tide lapped at the policemen's black boots. In another half an hour, his body would have been washed into the Atlantic just as Chris's dad had been. Was that what Pat had intended? The weather was too bad for any of the little fishing boats to venture out so none of the fishermen would have found him. He would have been washed out quietly and without fuss. It was deliberate.

*

Joe didn't need any help walking up the steps into the police station but Chris felt the need to touch him anyway, so put his hand on Joe's shoulder. They walked inside the foyer and approached the reception. "We're here to see PC Lewis."

The counter was high and there was clearly a plinth on the other side. It gave the receptionist an unnatural and overbearing height.

"Just take a seat and I'll put a call out for him."

They sat down and waited. The call went out and after a

few minutes, the officer appeared from a door to one side of the desk. He ushered them through and showed them to a room with *'Statement Taking Room'* stuck on the door. The notice was handwritten on a sheet of paper and taped in place. The officer shuffled the chairs around and sat on the opposite side with his computer. Only a third of his face was visible behind the monitor. There was no sympathy to be had here, only business.

Chris had only been in a police station three times and they were all following his dad's death. This wasn't the same place, he was sure if that. He remembered the other station as being castle-like and frightening, like something from a bad dream. This was much newer but no less dismal.

The officer took details about Pat, which Joe was able to give without thought or self-correction. The answer to his question about next of kin was sad. There was nobody. Joe was the closest thing Pat had to blood in the entire world.

"When will we be able to bury the lad?" Joe asked. His voice was steady but his face betrayed what was going on inside.

The officer stopped tapping on his keyboard, which he had been doing since they got there.

"In cases where suicide is suspected, the coroner will have an inquest, I'm afraid…"

"Suspected?" Joe exploded and stood up. He rummaged in his pocket and threw the soggy slip of paper on to the table. "I've got a pile of these this thick if you want to see them!" He spread his arms as wide as he could.

The officer slid the paper across and took an exhibit bag

from the drawer. He did his best to keep the paper flat but it was wet from the rain and finished up as a ball inside the bag.

"I understand and I'm sorry but it's the law."

Joe sat back down and rubbed his face. "Bugger the law," he whispered.

"How long will that take?" Chris put his hand over Joe's and looked to the officer.

He carried on typing. "It depends."

"On?" Chris asked.

He stopped typing and sighed. "On all sorts of things. I don't understand why these things take so long either. I'm sorry, I'm truly sorry I can't give you all the answers but the coroner is God." He opened the drawer again and produced a booklet which he pushed across the table. "This might help."

Joe took it and rolled it into a cone.

"So, when was the last time you saw Mr Bailey?" The officer looked at Joe but Chris answered.

"I saw him after my Granddad did. I went out with him last night."

Chris told the officer about meeting him in The Queen's Head and going for a drive afterwards. The officer had no idea who Jack Kestle was, but why would he? The man had died before the officer was even born. The officer took notes as Chris spoke, prompting him for more details here and there.

When it came to Pendeen, Chris kept the details short. They'd driven to the lighthouse and Pat had told him about the girls they used to take there when they were younger. Pat had drunk a couple of cans of cider in the car but nothing excessive. Chris didn't speak about what had happened there; what they had both seen. How could he talk about that? All the while, he could see Joe watching him.

"And then I took him home. I dropped him at the memorial anyway." He slid his hand off the table. His knuckle and fingers ached where he'd punched Pat. He saw Joe follow the movement of his hand.

"What time was that?"

Chris shrugged. He hadn't been keeping track of the time, especially after the incident at Pendeen. "About one-ish, I suppose."

"I heard you come in at about twenty past," Joe chimed in.

The officer nodded and wrote it down. "And how was he when you left him?"

Chris thought back to how things had been between them when Pat had walked off… piss down his legs and cider down his shirt.

"He was okay. He wasn't drunk, at least I've seen him much worse." He shrugged again. "He was okay."

"What did he say to you when he left?"

He said he was going to show me how to punch properly.

"Just that he'd see me tomorrow for a drink in the pub. That was all." He could feel his face reddening. It was as much from the situation, the pressure, the untruths he was speaking, as it was from the remorse that he'd started feeling. The last time he saw Pat, he just punched him in the face and had a row with him about…

"Okay, well I'll type this up and then ask you to sign it. Do you want to wait in here or out there?"

"How long will it take?" Joe asked.

"About half an hour or so." The officer was already typing on the computer again.

He looked at Joe who tilted his head toward the door. "Outside, I think."

The officer stood up and opened the door for them.

"Who told you he was there?" Joe asked.

The officer winced. "He did. He made the call himself. He said exactly what he'd written on the note, that he was sorry." After a pause, he added "I am sorry for your loss."

He shook his head and showed them out.

"Don't go too far." He nodded at the rain falling outside. "Not that you will."

Even though it was raining, they both stood outside and let the rain pelt their upturned faces. It cooled the skin on Chris's face immediately.

After a minute, Joe spoke. "We'll have a chat about that later."

Chris turned and looked at him. Joe's eyes were closed and the rain bounced off skin the colour of seasoned leather; a flesh formed by years of working under the Cornish sun. "Over a cup of tea, I think," he added.

Chris turned away and tipped his head back again. Joe knew when he was lying and he'd seen the signs in that little room.

The officer took them back into the room and pushed the statement paper across the table at Chris.

"Have a read of this, Mr Kestle, and if it's okay I'll show you where to sign. It's not as good as one of your stories I'm afraid, but then again it's not fiction is it?"

Chris smiled. He wasn't A-list by any means and he could count on the fingers of one hand the number of times he'd been recognised.

"Thank you." He started reading.

"Do either of you know if Mr Bailey had a partner? A girlfriend?"

Chris stopped reading. "I don't think so." He turned to Joe. "Do you?"

Joe shook his head. "Not that I know of. Nobody would have him. Why?"

"The operator who took the call thought she heard a voice in the background. A woman's voice shouting and screaming something. It was probably just the wind, it's pretty grim out there."

Chris finished reading the statement. "It's fine. Where do I need to sign?" He could feel his heart racing again as he heard himself ask "Um, this woman's voice... what was she saying?"

The officer leaned over the table and pointed at the various places for his signature. "Something about *seeing*, or *I see you*. Something like that, I don't know. They've listened to it again and there's nothing except for the wind." He took the statement off Chris and tapped the sheets together so they were tidy.

Chris felt sick. He could feel his stomach churning and the colour draining from his face. If he didn't get out of there, he was going to cover them all with soft-boiled eggs.

"They just wanted me to check with you." He stood up and opened the door. "That's it then. I've got your details for the coroner but we'll be in touch." He offered his hand to both of them and walked them to the door.

Chris had no idea how he was going to get down the steps. His legs felt as if they were made of jelly.

*

"I don't drink this neat before the moon rises, but today's different." Joe put the new bottle of Bushmills on the table with two tumblers. He poured two generous measures.

"Stand up, lad."

Chris stood up and took his glass. Joe was silent for a moment. For a man like him, who kept words to a minimum, finding the right ones was important. He stared into the space above Chris's head.

"I was his only family I suppose and now it's up to me to say something about him. That's how it should be." He swallowed and wiped his mouth. "I loved Pat Bailey like he was my own son. Not many people had a lot of time for him but a dad can forgive his son anything, anything at all. I loved him but I couldn't keep him safe." Joe raised his glass. "It's up to you to look after him now, Lord. Its up to you." He swallowed the measure in one and Chris did the same.

"Pat Bailey." They said it in unison.

They both sat down and for a long time there was silence.

Not even the sound of the rain on the windows or wind in the eaves could penetrate it. It was absolute to both of them.

Finally, Joe spoke. "So what's up with your hand then?"

Chris clenched it a couple of times. "Is it obvious?" His hand was sore but it wasn't swollen or discoloured.

"It wasn't. Not until you hid it under the table at the cop-shop when he asked you about Pat. You had a fight, didn't you?"

Chris exhaled loudly. Pat had killed himself, nobody else had done that, but there was a nasty little feeling of guilt scratching at the back of his neck.

"We did." He left it at that.

"I knew you weren't telling that copper everything. I could tell, I can always tell. What about? I've seen Pat argue over the toss of a coin but I ain't seen him fight too many times."

"He didn't fight, Granddad. At least he didn't fight back. I hit him and now I wish I could take it back." He paused. The image of Pat's forlorn figure trudging off into the night kept replaying in his mind. He couldn't tell Joe why they had fought any more than he could tell the copper. "We had a disagreement about something, nothing important really. Just something stupid."

"And you're not a fighter either. I don't need to see how sore your hand is to know that, Christopher." He got up from the table and walked toward the stairs. "I'm going for a lie down. When you're ready to tell me what the disagreement was about, I'll be listening."

Chris heard his footsteps on the stairs and then the sound

of his bedroom door closing. He sat and stared at his empty glass. Had Pat killed himself because of what he'd seen, what they had both seen, last night? No, it wasn't possible. Joe had talked about a drawer full of notes from Pat. He'd said there were lots of them. It was in his mind to cut his wrists long before last night.

How many times had Pat seen her? Afterwards he acted as if he'd just seen an old mate on the street, not a screaming banshee crawling all over the car, trying to get at him, trying to get at both of them.

Pat had tried to help him as best he could, by trying to bring him back to the car, by alerting him with the lights and the horn, but she had come down the slope. She had come for him, she wanted to push him over the cliff. She wanted to kill him. But the foghorn…

He clutched his head. It was all too much. What was he thinking? What was he considering here? Whatever had happened at Pendeen, she'd got one of them in the end. She hadn't pushed Pat over the cliff with her soulless eyes, but she had pushed him over the edge. The bloody stains on the slipway at Hawk's Cove would always show that. And now there were Pat's stains to add to his dad's.

Chapter 12

Chris knocked gently on Joe's door. He'd come up earlier but could hear him sobbing. He'd hovered at the door and listened for a moment then left. It wasn't that he was being heartless, just that he had a feeling this was something Joe needed to do on his own.

"Joe, I've made some chilli. Are you coming down?"

He heard some shuffling around coming from inside, then the door opened. Joe was dressed in what he called his *Sunday best*. It was a night for his tie.

"Good lad, I'm famished. Then we'll go to the pub and say goodbye to Pat to properly." He edged past Chris and started down the stairs. His bloodshot eyes hadn't escaped Chris's notice.

They both sat down and Joe immediately started shovelling the food into his mouth.

"Any good?" Chris asked.

Joe nodded and wiped his mouth on the paper napkin.

"Plenty of poke. Have we got any ale?" He put his head back down and carried on eating. Chris took this as a sign that it was good and fetched two bottles of beer. He knocked the caps off and put one next to Joe.

"Cheers." He tapped the bottles together and sat down.

"Cheers!" Joe held the bottle up and drank half of it in one go.

"Looks like there's plenty of poke in there, Granddad." He hadn't tasted his own yet but for Joe to take such a drink was unusual.

"There is, there certainly is, but tonight I'm getting drunk. Only been drunk once in the last thirty-three years and only once forty years before that. Tonight seems like the time has come again."

He put his head back down and picked up his fork. "You were too young for either of those so tonight you'll be joining me."

It wasn't a question. It was an instruction. Chris opened his mouth to offer an objection but realised it was pointless. Besides, it was actually a good idea.

He raised the bottle and took a long drink. "Well, I never got chance to get drunk with Dad so I'm with you all the way, Granddad."

Joe stopped eating for a moment. "One thing I'll need from you, though."

"Anything." He took a forkful of the chilli and felt an explosion in his mouth then his throat.

"Protection. I'll be needing protection."

Chris wiped his mouth and put his fork down. "Who from?"

"No, no. I'll need *you* to protect *them* from *me*."

Chris started to laugh but he could see Joe wasn't messing about. "Are you serious?"

Joe pushed more chilli in, swallowed it and then licked his lips. "When your dad died, it took seven of them to pull me off Jimmy Upson. He's long dead now but I would've killed him that night. I hit a few others too and poor old Pat caught one. It knocked him on his arse but he just got up and put his hand on my shoulder. He said, 'Joe, you've punched everyone in the pub now, there's nobody else left to hit. It's time to go home.'" He finished his beer. "It's been a while but I think I could have a row with someone tonight."

"Well, I better phone Ollie before things get out of hand."

"When am I going to see him again?"

"If it's okay with you…"

Joe raised his hand. "It's always okay with me."

"Then the week after next? Lou wants to talk to you first to make sure I'm not going to…" He didn't finish the sentence.

Joe looked up and smiled. The deep fissures on his skin, which he wore like scars, changed into a new pattern, a happy pattern.

"That's the best news I've had for a long time, Christopher. A very long time."

*

Chris kept it down to two bottles before he called Lou.

"Oh, Christ. How's Joe?" He'd just told her about Pat.

He closed the bedroom door. "I don't really know. He was in his room crying all afternoon but when he came out, he seemed fine. He wants to go to the pub and get drunk."

"Jesus." Lou's voice was breaking. "When I think what he's been through… I don't know how he carries on. He's lost so much." She paused. "Has Pat got *any* family?"

"Not a soul. Joe's as close to family as he's…" No, it wasn't present tense any longer. Pat was no longer *present*. "Joe was his family."

"When will they bury him?" Lou asked.

"They've got to have an inquest first and then who knows."

"Does that mean Joe will pay for the funeral?"

He hadn't thought about that at all. "I'll help him with that. If he wants me to."

There was a silence and then Lou spoke. "And what about you, Chris?"

That was a million dollar question if he'd ever heard one. How was he? "Look, I've found out some things about Dad and I've cleared the air with him, literally. There's things I need to say to you face to face but I'm getting there, Lou. I'm feeling better."

"I want you back, Chris. I want *you* back with me. It sounds like a silly cliché but I want things back to how they were."

Her voice was shaky but she wouldn't cry. She was too strong. It was she who had sent him away when she knew he wasn't right. She was the strong one and always had been.

"And I want to come back to you, Lou. More than

anything in the world I want to come back to you. I've spoken to Joe about half-term and you should've seen the look on his face." He could feel his own expression changing. "It made his year. Come to Cornwall, Lou. Bring Ollie and let's forget this year ever happened. We can do it. I can do it."

"I'm not going to rush into it. You've got to be honest with me and when we talk you have to tell me everything. You need to open up and let it all out. I'm here for you, I've always been here for you but you won't allow me to help. I won't see Ollie like he was after the party. I won't, Chris. I won't do it."

Thinking about that was almost too much. Ollie standing there reciting the book they had both loved when he was a toddler should have been framed in a glorious, golden light inside his head, on centre stage. Instead it was tainted by what had happened. He'd shoved it to the back of his mind, along with the things he didn't want to think about. *She* was in there too, but she was barging her way to the front and he couldn't stop her. Neither, it seemed, could Pat.

"And you're right. He comes first in all of this, he comes first. I've got a bit of a plan about these nightmares and don't shoot me down straight away. Okay?"

He heard her sigh. "I'll listen to anything if it means I can get a few hours sleep. It's like when he was a baby again. Can you remember that? We didn't get any sleep for two years. It feels like that again, but worse."

"Okay, well how about this? He has your mobile through

the night and if he gets scared or has a nightmare, he just calls me. Put it on speed-dial or whatever you call it now." He was useless with his phone. He knew how to text and how to make calls, other than that, all the icons were just garish coloured squares on the screen.

"You speak to him about it first though. I don't want him messing about with it."

He thought it was a good idea but he hadn't expected Lou to go for it straight away. "Of course I will. Is he there? I know it's not bedtime yet but I'll need to go with Joe and look after him." That was a lie but he didn't need to tell Lou the full story.

"I'll fetch him." There was a pause and then a muffled call for Ollie.

"He's on his way."

"Lou? I love you."

"I love you, Chris. Just get better. Here he is."

"Hi, Dad."

"Hey big man. How was school?"

"Alright." When it came to school, Ollie was a man of few words.

"Have you done your homework?"

"Dad? You know on Minecraft, I've built this really, really high tower and at the top I've built a lookout so we can see if any creepers come so we can shoot them with the bow and arrow. It's on the world we created. I'll show you when you come home."

The question about homework was as unimportant as was the question about school.

"Sounds good to me. I just want to have a quick chat about tonight and then you can carry on with Minecraft, okay?" There was silence on the other end.

"Ollie, it's important and you might like it?"

"Okayyyyyy."

"What if you had Mum's phone tonight?"

"What? All night?" He sounded excited now.

"Yes, all night. But you can only use it if you get scared or you've had a bad dream. Then, instead of waking Mum up, you just phone me? It doesn't matter what time it is or if you're just a little bit scared. You just press the button and I'll be listening. How does that sound?"

"It sounds good. I bet I can get YouTube on Mum's phone, I can watch…"

"No, Ollie, you can't get YouTube on Mum's phone…"

"You can." It was Ollie's turn to interrupt. "You can get it on yours too. I watched a whole episode of Scooby-Doo on there once. It was small but I could still see everything."

Ollie wanted to talk about anything except bedtime and bad dreams, which was perfectly understandable.

"Have we got a plan then?"

"Yep, I'll phone you when I get scared. But Dad?"

"Yes, Ollie." He was expecting some more comments about Minecraft or YouTube.

"What do I do if I need a cuddle?"

Chris bit his lip hard. Hard enough to draw blood. "Well, then you'll just have to go and climb into bed with Mum and wrap your arms around her. Keep my spot nice and warm, eh?"

"Okay, Dad. I'm excited about coming to see Lollipop."

"He is too! He said it would make his year."

"I can't wait." He was onto the next thing already but that was good. It was *normal* Ollie.

"I've got to go now but remember what we talked about. Yes?"

"I'll phone you if I'm scared."

"That's it. I'll see you soon, okay big man? I love you."

"I love you too."

Then was the sound of muffled voices and the phone went dead. Ollie knew how to use the phone better than he did but Lou would make sure the phone was ready to call him in the night.

He took a deep breath. He couldn't actually be with Ollie but the phone was the next best thing. It was a poor substitute but at least it was something.

"Are you ready?" Joe's voice called up to him.

He opened the bedroom door and walked down the stairs. "We'll drive up and leave the car there. I'll pick it up in the morning."

"Whatever you say." Joe was already halfway out of the house. There were another two empty bottles of beer on the table. Was it possible, or even safe, for a man of Joe's age to drink so much? Chris wasn't sure but he certainly wasn't going to ask those questions.

*

The Queen's Head never seemed to be full. It was always busy but because there were various rooms, it never felt overloaded. In the summer months, people sometimes had to wait a few minutes before they were served but that was about as bad as things got. Mostly, it was a comfortable place to go and have a quiet drink. If someone from the village had died, it was a different matter. Then it was packed to the rafters. Tonight was a night during which Susie Curnow would need not just one extra pair of hands but several.

As Chris parked the car and turned off the engine, the sound of a gathered crowd rumbled out of the pub and into the car.

"There's a few in tonight." Joe climbed out of the car.

There were people standing outside the pub smoking and as they passed, each of them shook Joe's hand and patted him on the back. Chris had never seen any of them before but they shook his hand too.

The pub might have been packed and the noise loud, but it wasn't a happy sound. There was no laughter mixed in with the usual hum of chatter. It was low-pitched and hollow, and when Joe came in, it went down to another level.

He marched straight over to the bar where Susie was waiting. His gleaming shoes made a metallic clicking sound with each step. She opened her mouth to speak but Joe silenced her with a wave of his hand.

"Say what you want in a minute, lovely, but right now, me and my lad here want two pints of Tribute." He reached into his pocket and withdrew a fold of notes. Chris couldn't see how much was there but it was a thick fold.

"And when we've done with the first two we'll need some

more please. And if there's enough left over when I've had enough, I'd like everyone to wish my other lad, Patrick Bailey, a safe trip to the next place with a glass in their hands. And I'd like to buy you one too. In fact I'd like you to keep yourself in drinks all night."

Susie took Joe's money and put it in a tin behind the bar. "I'll keep it safe here." She pulled them two pints and before the glass had landed on the wooden bar-top, Joe had it in his hand.

"This one's just between you and me, son. Here's to Pat."

Chris took his glass and knocked it against Joe's. "Pat." They both took a drink and smiled at each other.

It wasn't long before someone had pulled a stool up at the bar for Joe. He had pulling power anyway but today it was magnified a hundred times and it wasn't just his offer of free beer either. The whole village knew Joe and he knew everyone who lived there. This made them as close as family. Not that they were all friends, being part of a family doesn't make you friends, but they knew each other's business. They all knew Pat and they all knew what role Joe had played in Pat's life.

He nodded and smiled. He hugged and he bit his lip to stop the tears flowing. He even made several mini-speeches and toasts, but through it all he drank. He drank like a man who hadn't tasted beer for a hundred years.

Chris tried his best to keep up with him. and for the most part he did. He even put another fifty pounds behind the bar. But Joe had asked Chris to do a job for him and he wanted to stay in control.

He left Joe for a short time and went to the toilet but as he walked back toward the bar, he could hear Joe's voice raised above the chatter.

"Well, he didn't much care for you either, Dave, so I think I'll have that back off you."

As Chris reached the bar, Joe was trying to take a pint out of someone's hand. The other man didn't want to let go.

Joe hadn't stood up for three hours, not even to empty his bladder, but he got to his feet now and was as steady as a rock.

"David Tallack, you are going to give me that back or I am going to knock you on your arse." Joe put his own pint down on the bar.

Chris didn't feel too steady on his feet, less steady than Joe appeared to be anyway, but he knew this wasn't an idle threat. Joe's words echoed in his ears. *I'll need you to protect them from me.*

He looked at the other man, who was closer to his age than Joe's. The last thing anyone wanted was for this to turn into a brawl but Joe wouldn't back down, he knew that for sure.

Chris intervened, smiled at Tallack. "Just give it him back, it's not the right time to be arguing about…"

"And who are you?" Tallack cut him off.

"He's my lad, that's who he is." Joe still had hold of Tallack's pint.

Tallack looked Chris up and down and turned back to Joe. "That ain't your lad. Your lad topped himself down at Hawk's Cove, just like Bailey."

Chris wasn't holding onto a pint, he wasn't holding anything in his hand except for a ball of rage. He closed his fingers around it and punched David Tallack in the face as hard as he could. He wasn't aiming for any particular part but the explosion of blood and the crunch of bone told him he'd hit the nose. There was nothing now, not the sound of talking or of glasses chinking behind the bar, just the roar of blood in his ears. Just the sound of rage.

Tallack fell back. If it weren't for the number of people standing behind him, he would have fallen over.

Chris stepped forward and drew back his fist. This time he took deliberate aim and hit him in the eye. Tallack went back again but the crowd had parted and he fell against the bar.

"My dad…" Chris drew back his fist and punched him in the other eye. He felt a bone give. Whether it was Tallack's eye socket or part of his own fist, he didn't really care.

"Did not…" He hit his eye again. Tallack didn't raise his hands to defend himself and in the back of Chris's head someone was shouting, "Stop, stop, stop!"

"Top himself!" He took Tallack by his collar and looked into his eyes. The man stared back at him, he was senseless.

Chris felt his own collar being tugged and then his arms being pulled back. He expected someone to start on him, maybe one of Tallack's mates, but he was just pulled backwards away from Tallack.

"Drink this and then it's time you were off." Someone tried to put a glass in his right hand but he couldn't bend his fingers. They pushed it into his left hand instead.

He looked down at it and then looked around the room. That brief moment of madness was already turning into a dream. Joe was sitting back on his stool, calmly finishing his pint. There was no crowd around him now and people were filing quickly out of the pub.

He turned to whoever it was had pushed the drink into his hand. It was Susie. "I… er…"

"Don't fret, Chris. We'll sort it." She smiled at him and walked over to Tallack who was standing with two other members of staff. They were pushing red paper napkins onto his face.

"Come on then, boy. Time we were off." Joe stood up and stretched his back. "I've had my fill."

Chris downed the drink. The brandy wasn't the finest Cognac, that was for sure, but it brought him back round. He looked at Tallack again. He should apologise to the man. He hadn't punched anyone since school and now he'd done it to two different men in less than twenty-four hours. It had felt good though, hadn't it? Not last night with Pat, that was different, but hitting Tallack felt like he'd let something out that needed to be released. Oh, it had felt good. Very, very good.

"Don't worry, Joe. We'll take care of this." Susie dabbed a napkin at Tallack's nose and turned around.

Joe reached into his pocket and pulled out only the cotton liner. He shrugged. "And I'm much obliged to you."

Chris walked over to the bar and put his last twenty pound note down. He avoided the congealing blood.

Joe patted him on the shoulder as they walked outside.

"Feels better, doesn't it?"

Chris took a deep breath of the cool night air. "What, getting pissed, or belting someone?" He wanted to vomit.

"You didn't just belt him, you *collided* with him. That's what you needed. You're angry, Christopher, you're very angry and you've every right to be. Just like me. Watching you do that to him was… it was therapeutic." He took a deep breath and started walking across the square. "We better get moving before it starts raining again."

Chris watched him for a moment. Joe was right, he was angry and Tallack had taken that anger with full force.

"Hold up!" he called after him. His legs felt like jelly again and the skin on his fist felt like it didn't fit properly anymore. The alcohol was numbing the pain but he couldn't bring himself to look at it. That would come in the morning when his head would hurt just as much. He set off after Joe.

It wasn't long before they were walking in complete darkness. They wobbled along the lane together, listening to the sound of the wind blowing through the hedgerow and the occasional scurry of a small animal running for its life in the undergrowth. There was no moon but Joe had walked this lane every day for years, he didn't need any lights to guide him home.

"You saved me a job," he said after a while.

"A job?"

"Sorting that Tallack idiot out. If you hadn't got him first, I was ready." Joe shook his fist. Over ninety or not, Chris wouldn't want to be on the receiving end of a punch from him.

"Well, he got what he was asking for." Chris tried to clench his fist and winced. "I went too far though, I didn't want to…"

"You wanted to kill him, just like I wanted to kill Jimmy Upson. Sometimes the human spirit needs to escape. You can't keep it locked up inside this bag of bones forever, you know. Sometimes it needs to come rushing out and belt the living daylights out of someone. Someone like Tallack or Upson. I got the pint back too. The bugger weren't having that."

Chris sniggered and then Joe started too. They both stopped walking and laughed like a pair of idiots. Joe was bent over clutching his knees.

"I need to piss," Joe said and tottered over to the hedge.

Chris exhaled and tasted the nutty beer fumes again. His head wasn't just going to hurt in the morning, it was going to pound.

"I could do with one too." He walked over to the hedge and stood a few paces away from Joe.

"When Jack used to come to the pub with me, we used to have a little competition on the way back."

"What was that?" Chris asked.

"Who could hold it the longest. Not once did either of us make it all the way home but your dad made it all the way to Jenner's place once. You should've seen the way he was walking."

Joe started laughing again. Jenner owned the first house on the row of terraces Joe lived on. Two miles with a full bladder was good going.

"Mostly though," Joe continued, "we'd stop about here and siphon it off." Joe zipped his trousers back up and pointed down the lane, into the darkness. "Course, we'd have to stop again, down there, and then further down the…" He stopped, frozen in mid-comment, with his finger pointing into the blackness.

"Granddad?" Chris buttoned up.

Joe moved his hand slowly toward his cap. He raised the brim and nodded. It was the same gesture as he'd made at the cemetery.

"Granddad? Who are you looking at it?" Chris felt his heart rate go up a notch. He followed Joe's gaze but there was nothing, nothing except the silhouette of a tree.

"Looks like she's come out for a stroll tonight. Not seen her down here before."

"Lizzy?" He moved closer to Joe who was still staring toward the tree. His frown was noticeable even in the darkness.

"Wonder what brings her down here?" Joe's voice was little more than a whisper.

"I can't see anything, just the tree."

"Well maybe you're not looking in the right place. She's there alright and she doesn't look happy."

"Maybe it's because we drank too much?"

"Maybe." Joe tipped his hat again. "Night, gal." He started walking again.

Chris squinted into the darkness for a second and looked away quickly. Lizzy might be there somewhere in the gloom but other things lurked in there too; things with eyes that had nothing but death and despair in their blackened voids.

"We better get a march on, it's going to rain in a minute." Joe was already walking quickly but he upped his pace a little more.

Chris couldn't feel any rain on his face but he didn't want to disagree with Joe. His mood had changed immediately and the lines on his face looked to have grown deeper. If that was at all possible.

Chapter 13

Chris climbed into bed. Joe had been almost silent for the rest of the walk home and hadn't even wanted a night-cap. Chris hadn't pushed it, he could see that Joe looked troubled. That had been emphasised by the expression on his face when they stepped into the lit kitchen. He looked old. He *was* old but he actually looked it tonight and that alone was a worry for Chris.

The room wasn't spinning, the walk home had stopped that from happening, but the sour and dry taste in his mouth was an indication of what was to come in the morning. He closed his eyes and saw the bloody pulp he'd made of Tallack's face. He had no idea he had the capacity to do that to someone, to carry on hitting them even when they were beaten. Even when they were defenceless.

He stretched his arm out from beneath the duvet and checked his phone. It was on and the volume was turned up to the maximum. If Ollie needed him, he'd be ready.

*

The rain was hammering on the window. It was so loud it was keeping him awake. Christ, it was so heavy it might actually smash the window. He lay there for a moment and listened. The sound of rain was supposed to be calming, relaxing and sleep-inducing. This wasn't though, this was more like drumming, loud incessant drumming and it was becoming deafening.

He wriggled to the side of the bed closest to the window and reached out. The glass was cold; droplets of moisture were forming on the inside. It was double-glazed but the rain was so heavy it was coming through. Actually coming through the glass.

He stood up, cupped his hands around his face and looked out. The darkness was absolute, as it should be. He could almost make out the shadow of the group of trees in the bottom field, but other than that there was nothing.

Except, the darkness was on two levels. There was black and then there was *black*. One above the other and the higher level was moving toward him, toward the cottage. It was a cloud, a massive storm cloud. How much heavier could the rain get? Panic started to rise and he immediately felt silly. But the drumming sound was getting closer. With each beat of his heart, there were three coming from the… not from the rain but from the cloud.

His hands weren't just damp now, water was actually dripping from them and running down his wrists, forearms and then onto his naked torso. The water was cold, icy cold.

Water dripped from his brow as if he'd just finished a session in the gym. It fell over his lips and dripped into his mouth. It was salty. How could that be? How could there be salt water dripping down the inside of the window? It wasn't just dripping though, it was running down the glass in great, black streaks.

But the drumming was getting faster and faster and the great blackness that was approaching was almost on top of the cottage. There was no differing levels of darkness now, the cloud filled the sky. There was no moon, there were no stars, just the darkness.

Now it was closer, he could see it moving. It was rolling like… like a great wave, a tsunami. It wouldn't just destroy the house, the row of cottages, it would take the whole village with it too. He had to move and warn Joe. He had to warn the whole village. But it was too late. The wave was upon him now. It barrelled toward the cottage in a great swarming barrel of energy.

Water ran down his face in a river, and beneath his feet he could feel the icy cold that only seawater can bring. It rose to his knees, his waist and now it was on his chest. The pressure was immense, squeezing him like a belt, trying to deprive him of his breath. And now it was over his mouth but he couldn't move, he was trapped. He was going to drown, right here in Joe's bedroom.

The wave was above him, it was cresting and when it came down it would crush him, just as it should have done all those years ago. But there had been someone to save him then, hadn't there? Dad wasn't here now. There was just him and the drumming. The loud and incessant drumming, beating so fast it made his heartbeat sound lazy.

Just as the wave turned, he saw her. Her eyes were bottomless pools of water. Her expression was vile and depraved. She looked down on him from the maelstrom of foaming darkness as the wave finally fell on him, and laughed. He couldn't hold his breath any longer. He would fill his lungs with salt water, no longer would he have to look into those eye sockets and see the hideous despair and anger.

"I can see you," she whispered.

He opened his mouth to shout back at her, anything would do, but all he did was inhale the water.

The drumming, the drumming, the drumming. She was coming, closer and closer.

*

He lurched forward in bed and retched. His heart was hammering in his chest but at least it was beating. He inhaled deeply and felt the air fill his lungs. It felt as if he'd been holding his breath as he slept.

At least the drumming sound had stopped. Was that her heartbeat, was that what it was? He felt his skin. It was damp but *sweaty* damp, not how his flesh had felt on the day they pulled him…

He pushed it aside. That was a box he couldn't open. Not yet, not in the dead of night after a nightmare.

He jumped and emitted an involuntary grunt as the drumming sound started again. The corner of the room beside the bed glowed. The drumming was the sound of the phone vibrating on the bedside table.

He grabbed it quickly and briefly saw Lou and Ollie smiling back at him on the screen before he swiped his finger across to accept the call. He'd had the phone on vibrate, not sound. *Shit.*

There was silence on the other end.

"Ollie?" He could hear his own heartbeat next to the sound of his son's name. It tapped out a horrible percussion.

"Ollie, are you there?" He probably had the phone next to him in bed and rolled on it or something. Chris would speak to him in the morning and make sure he put it at the bottom of the bed. He checked the time. It was just after two o'clock. Another three hours and Joe would be up for his walk.

"Dad?" Ollie's voice was barely a whisper.

"I'm here, you okay?" He whispered too.

"Dad, I'm scared. I'm really scared." Ollie was close to tears.

"It's okay, it's okay, I'm here. Bad dream?"

"I had a dream about you, Dad. Another dream about you. You were at the bottom of the sea. You're okay, aren't you? You're alive, aren't you?" Ollie was now sobbing but very quietly.

"Hey, hey, hey, listen, I'm fine. I'm absolutely fine."

"But you didn't answer your phone, you didn't answer it and I thought… I dreamed about it."

Chris cursed himself. He should have checked then double-checked but he'd been too pissed and too tired.

"I'm sorry, Ollie, I'm really sorry. I was…" *Having a*

nightmare myself. "I'd put my phone on vibrate and…"

"She's here." Ollie lowered his voice again and in the background Chris could hear muffled sounds of the duvet being tugged.

"Is it Mum?"

"I'm under the covers, she can't see me."

"Ollie? Let Mum give you a cuddle, it's okay."

"It isn't Mum." His voice shook slightly but he wasn't weeping any more.

This was just a hangover from the dream. Lou said it took a while for him to come out of them.

"Ollie, it's okay. There's nobody there. There's nobody else in the room."

"She's standing in the corner but I can't see her properly. Dad, I'm scared, I'm scared."

"Ollie, listen to me. There's nobody else in your room. It's all just part of the bad dream, there's nothing to be afraid of and I'm absolutely fine."

There was a noise in the background, like something being dragged. He was at the end of what he could do.

"I think Mum might have a cuddle waiting for you if you climb into our bed. Remember what I said about keeping my side warm for me."

"Dad, I can hear her breathing. She's right over me. Dad, Dad, Dad!" Ollie screamed.

As clear as a bell, *her* hissing voice came down the phone.

"I can see you."

Chris felt like he wasn't in his own body anymore. He was plastered to the ceiling, looking down at himself; unable to move and utterly useless.

He pushed the phone against his ear until he felt pain. On the other end was the muffled sound of movement, of rapid and panicked movement. And of sobbing, of restrained but continual sobbing.

"Ollie, Ollie!" Chris shouted but Ollie had dropped the phone. He could hear him scrambling around his bed.

What could he do? Why was she there? Why was *she* there with his son? "Get away from him!"

Then there were footsteps and a piercing scream that pushed the phone away from his ear. He'd heard that scream before in the delivery suite at the hospital. It was Lou.

"Lou, Lou! What's going on?"

He was panicking. At some point he'd climbed out of bed and was pacing up and down the room.

"Lou!" he shouted as loudly as he could.

Then there was silence. He stared at the screen to make sure he still had a connection. Lou was standing next to Ollie in the dappled sunshine of an afternoon spent walking in the woods. They were both laughing after he'd told a terrible joke.

"Oh, God. Oh God, Chris." Lou's voice was closer to a breath than speech.

"Lou?" He tried to keep his own voice level but he knew it didn't sound that way. "Lou, you have to tell me what's happening there."

There was just heavy breathing coming from the other end.

"Lou! What is it?" He was shouting now but he didn't

care. He had to know what the hell was going on.

"There was... it was standing over... I don't know..." She stopped. In the background he could hear Ollie wailing. It was hellish.

"Lou! Hold it together, just hold it together for Ollie."

There was a pause. "Chris, I don't know what happened. I don't... I don't know what it was. I don't understand what I saw. It can't... It wasn't there, it couldn't be but I saw it. I saw *her*."

Chris felt cold all over. He was back in the sea on that day, on the day when he'd felt the life being sucked out of him by the numbing water.

Lou was right, it wasn't possible. None of it was possible but it was happening anyway.

"I need you to do something for me, Lou. I need you to tell me exactly what it was you saw. Exactly." He knew what it was. He'd seen her for himself but with Pat gone, there was nobody else to confirm it. Nobody else to tell him he wasn't seeing things. He could hear Ollie taking short breaths and then groaning. Lou was with him again.

"Chris, I can't, it wasn't real."

"Mum! She is real, I tried to tell you last night and the night before, she is real and she keeps coming to my room." Ollie was crying but he wasn't hysterical. He should have been if what was in Chris's mind was the same thing as he'd actually just been through.

"It doesn't make sense, it's not real." Lou was steady but shock was clearly setting in. She was trying to make sense of it. She was trying to come to terms with what had just happened. Ollie, it seemed, was already at that stage.

"Her eyes…" Lou stopped there. It was enough. He'd heard enough.

"Lou?"

There was a grunt from the other end which he took as an acknowledgement.

"Lou, I want you to pack a bag. I want you to pack bags for both of you and I want you to get in the car and come here."

"But… but…"

"You don't wait until the morning, you just pack and get in the car now. Did you hear me?" Even if he could get her in the car, was she safe to drive?

He could still hear Ollie in the background. He was still sobbing but the gaps between the ascending intakes of breath were getting longer.

"Lou, get in that fucking car and drive." As bad as things had been between them, he had never spoken to her like that in his life. He would never dream of it, she'd kick his balls all the way to the moon if he did. He hoped it would shock her out of the dazed state she was in.

"I'll get the bags." She paused and then repeated it again. "I'll get the bags and come. I'm doing it now."

"There she is, you're back with me. Now, pass the phone to Ollie while you pack. I'll talk to him. Okay?"

"Yes, yes. Five minutes and we'll be in the car." A pause and then she passed the phone to Ollie. "It's Dad again, just talk to him."

"Dad, I'm scared. Is she coming back again? She's…"

He'd stopped crying, which was at least something.

"Ollie, slow down. Mum's packing and you're coming to Lollipop's."

"What? Now?"

"Yes, now, right now. Okay? You'll be safe here, I promise."

Ollie started crying again. "But Dad, what if she gets us on the way? What if she gets Mum?"

"She isn't going to get anyone. She isn't..." He was going to say *real* but they both knew this was a lie. She might not be flesh and blood like everyone else but she was real, and she was dangerous.

"...Going to hurt you. I'll talk to you all the way if you like? You can just talk to me while Mum drives."

"Yes please Dad. Dad, don't leave us again."

Chris felt a huge knot in his throat. It threatened to tighten on his voice box. "Never, ever, Ollie. Never ever again."

He could hear Lou opening and closing drawers and cupboards in the background and then her voice came through. It sounded clear and controlled. That was good. "Ollie, time to go!"

"Dad, it's dark outside, I don't want to go where it's dark."

"It's okay, if you just grab Gerald in one hand and Mum's hand in the other and then close your eyes, Mum will get you both in the car and lock the doors."

"But she can get through locked doors!" Ollie shouted. "I've already told Mum that!"

"Not when Mum's driving at a hundred miles an hour she can't."

He had no idea if that was true or not but staying put wasn't an option.

"Mum wants you."

"Chris, we're packed and ready. We'll be with you as quickly as I can get there."

"Good, Ollie's going to talk to me on the phone all the way. Just get here safely."

"Okay, okay." She sounded out of breath. "Ollie, come on. Talk to Dad again."

Chris talked Ollie to the car. In his mind he saw Ollie with one hand wrapped around the phone and Gerald the giraffe's floppy neck, and the other tightly held in Lou's hand. He talked him into the front seat and carried on as Lou reversed off the drive and started the journey they all knew so well. They talked about everything. They talked about anything. Anything except what had just happened.

After a couple of hours discussing Minecraft, dinosaurs, space and the beach at Gwynver, Ollie's speech started to slow down. His words became more frequently interspersed with yawns.

"I'm tired, Dad, I might have a sleep."

"That's a good idea. Can you pass me over to Mum before you do, please? By the time you wake up, you'll be here and I'll be waiting."

Ollie let out a contented sigh.

"I'm here." Lou sounded rock-steady. Chris could count on the fingers of one hand when she had been anything but in their entire relationship.

"Where are you?"

"We've just gone past Bristol so, what… another three hours?"

Chris checked the time on his screen. That meant they would be with him by eight-thirty.

"Want me to stay on the line with you?" he asked.

"I'll be okay. I need to concentrate on driving. You normally do this and I'm doing it from memory so I need to be in one place and that's in the car with my hands around the wheel. If we start talking, I'll be somewhere else and I don't want to go there alone with just my little boy in the car. Make sense?"

"Of course it does. I'll be waiting for you but call me if there are any problems. Anything, Lou."

"Absolutely."

"I love you."

"I love you too. I'll see you in a few hours." She ended the call.

Chris stared at the screen until it dimmed out and then looked across the room at the window. He'd gone to bed without drawing the curtains but there was little point now. Besides, he didn't like the idea of walking over there and closing them. He might see a tidal wave coming toward the house with a virago riding the crest and hissing those horrible words at him.

He sat on the bed, deliberately turning his back to the window. How could this all be rationalised? It was a stupid question because none of it could really be happening.

According to everyone – the police, Joe, everyone – the woman had never been on the slipway on that day. But he'd seen her. He hadn't stopped seeing her.

Pat had pretended that he hadn't seen her and yet he had. And he had seen her before. How many times was now impossible to know, but he'd seen her before, that much was obvious.

And now Ollie had seen her, she had been in his room. She had done God knew what to him but Lou had seen her too now. She was everywhere and it seemed he was the only connection to it all. She was coming for him. She was going to take everyone he loved with her.

"What's going on?" The bedroom door swung open and Joe shuffled in. "Put some clothes on, lad. I don't want to see any of that." He turned away. He was wrapped in a great blue and green tartan dressing gown. It had been a Christmas present from Ollie last year and there had been a mistake with the order. As a result it was at least two sizes two large but he refused to have it exchanged.

Chris realised he'd been naked throughout it all; naked and pacing up and down the room. He grabbed yesterday's boxers from the side of the bed and slipped them on. "Sorry, Granddad." He rubbed his hands over his hair and stretched his back. "Would it be a problem if Lou and Ollie came a bit sooner than planned?"

"No. No problem at all. They could come this morning if it was down to me."

Chris stood up and pulled his jeans on. "I'm pleased you said that. They'll be here in about three hours."

Joe smiled, a great beaming smile that smoothed away all his worry lines in an instant.

"I best get some more eggs then. Ollie likes a boiled egg for his breakfast." He walked out of the room.

It was still dark outside but he could hear Joe getting ready for his walk. In another hour, dawn would break and this night would feel like a nightmare. He grabbed his partially buttoned shirt, which was also abandoned next to the bed, and pulled it on. He had a feeling that although the night was over, the nightmare was far from finished. Very far.

Chapter 14

Chris stood on the lane and waited. It was raining, not hard, but his hair and shirt were wet. It was gone nine. He'd tried to phone Lou an hour ago to check on her progress but the phone went straight to voicemail. It wouldn't be a surprise if the battery died, given how long he was on the line with Ollie for, but it wasn't doing his nerves any good.

He looked over his shoulder. Joe was standing at the kitchen window trying to look like he was washing pots, but there weren't any. He was waiting too. Joe hadn't asked why Lou was driving to Cornwall in the middle of the night but that was nothing unusual. He didn't start conversations with a *why,* that wasn't his way. It wasn't his business, but once that door was open and the invite handed to him, he would step inside and give whatever assistance was needed. Right now, he was just happy that his great-grandson was coming to stay. If there were questions, they would come later when Chris or Lou were happy to open that door.

He looked up the lane again. Where were they? The Highways Agency was always tinkering with the A30, particularly during the summer, but he didn't see any major works on the way down.

He hadn't listened to the local radio though. Joe had listened to the shipping forecast as usual but not local radio.

"Come on, come on," he whispered and saw the first traces of vapour coming from his mouth. He didn't feel cold but it was the adrenalin that was keeping him warm. Autumn was here and it could be spiky as well as beautiful.

He looked over his shoulder again, making a *where are they?* gesture with his hands to Joe. The rain started falling heavier but he wouldn't go back inside until they were here. He cocked his ear, something he'd been doing for the last hour, and listened. Was that a car? The other false alarms had been the wind or the echo of his heartbeat in his ears.

It was a car. It was definitely a car. He took a few steps forward then around the bend came Lou's black C-Max. He jumped in the air with relief and turned to give Joe the thumbs-up. Joe returned the gesture.

Chris backed away to give Lou the space to turn the car onto the patch of grass next to the cottage. He could see Ollie's head lolling to one side. He was still asleep but as the car came to a stop, his eyes opened. For a brief moment there was panic in his expression. As soon as he saw Chris, the panic vanished and a huge smile spread over his face.

Lou smiled too, but hers wasn't the unrestrained glee of Ollie's. It was an expression of relief.

"Dad!" Ollie jumped out of the car and wrapped his arms

around Chris's waist. His capacity to go from zero to one hundred in less than a second was amazing. Ollie wasn't big on hugging, not unless it was on his terms. And as for kisses, well they just got wiped off with an expression of disgust.

Chris lifted him, planted a kiss on each of his cheeks then one on his forehead. He didn't make a move to wipe them away this time.

"I told you I'd be here when you woke up." It felt good to hold Ollie again, even though his arms were aching at the weight.

"Is Lollipop here?"

Chris squeezed him then put him down. His hand was raging with the pain of last night's brawl but it paled beside Ollie. "Look over there." Ollie was too small to see over the top of the car but Joe was waiting in the doorway.

Ollie ran around the car and shouted "Lollipop!" at the top of his voice. He hurled himself into Joe's arms, just as Chris had done at the same age. He could feel the tears building in his eyes and bit down on his lip to stop them coming.

Lou was watching them from her side. Chris walked around the car and joined her. He put his hand on her arm. "Okay?"

There was no blinking away the tears that rolled down her cheeks. She fell into his arms and he wrapped them around her. He held her close, feeling her sobs shuddering through her body. He had to be strong again, for both of them. She couldn't carry him anymore. He held her that way until the rain dripped from his hair and his shirt clung to his body.

"Let's go inside," he whispered into her ear.

She nodded and took his hand.

Joe was already pouring tea for them when they walked through the door. "Ollie's gone upstairs and he's putting Gerald to bed."

Lou walked over and hugged him. "I'm sorry we've just descended on you like this, it…"

Joe held his hand up. "You could stay here forever for me."

Lou planted a kiss on his cheek and hugged him again. "You are a very special man, Joseph Kestle, and I love you for taking care of my man here."

Her voice was wavering again and Joe passed her a sheet of kitchen towel.

"I don't carry handkerchiefs anymore so this is the best I can do." He passed her a mug of tea. "You can take that upstairs and get into bed. We'll sort the little man out, don't you worry about that."

Lou took it and looked at Chris. "I'm shattered."

He nodded toward the stairs. "You heard the man. Go on." She stared back at him with a look that he knew very well. It was a look usually reserved for when she wanted to talk to him out of Ollie's earshot.

"It looks like I'll have to follow her up and make sure she sticks to orders then." He turned around but Joe was already boiling an egg for Ollie's breakfast. He didn't want to mention it but Ollie had stopped eating 'dippy' eggs earlier in the year. He followed Lou upstairs.

"Ollie, come and give Mum a kiss, she's going to bed for

a while." He peeked into Ollie's room. He was clutching Gerald and staring out of the window.

Ollie turned and ran out of his room clutching the giraffe. Chris had a feeling Gerald wouldn't be too far from Ollie's side for a while.

He kissed Lou and rushed off back downstairs. The excitement of being at Lollipop's had pushed any other feelings to the back of his mind. It was good but it wouldn't last forever and tonight might bring a fresh challenge for him.

Lou was undressing. She looked weary and it wasn't just last night's drive that had done that to her. The last few nights had obviously been tough but there was a year of Chris's deteriorating behaviour backing that up.

"Do you want something to eat?" he asked.

She shook her head and pulled the duvet over her body.

"No, I'm not hungry. We need to phone school and tell them Ollie's sick. I can phone work later. This is my side, why does it smell of you?"

He sat on the edge of the bed and brushed her fringe away from her eyes. "I'll sort school." He stopped and kissed her forehead. "I'm sorry." It felt like he'd been saying that a lot recently.

"I know you are." She smiled up at him. It was thin but at least it was there. It slipped away slowly. "Last night…"

He kissed her on the lips this time. It was as much a sign of affection as it was to stop her saying anything else on the subject. "We'll talk later. Just try and sleep."

"Just stay until I drop off."

She closed her eyes and he stayed with her for a few minutes until he could feel her body twitching. He kissed her head again and she murmured something and rolled over.

When he got downstairs, Ollie was tucking into his boiled egg and soldiers. Joe was sitting on the opposite end of the table watching him.

"I didn't think you liked them anymore?" He ruffled Ollie's hair as he walked past him to collect his tea.

"I don't like *your* dippy eggs. Lollipop's are different, they taste nice." He had egg yolk on his chin and smears of Cornish butter on each of his cheeks.

"So I can see."

"You look shattered too, lad. Why don't you go and get some rest? Me and Ollie will be just fine. Won't we?"

Ollie nodded his head.

Chris did feel exhausted, he'd been up most of the night too but seeing Ollie and Lou had charged his batteries a bit.

"I thought we might look for some crabs down at Sennen. Anyone fancy that?"

Ollie turned so quickly he almost fell off the chair. "Can we go surfing, too?"

Chris looked out of the window. It was raining, not hard, but incessant.

"Well, I've got a fiver burning a hole in my pocket for a new crab-line and a bucket," Joe said just at the right time.

Ollie turned back to Joe. His eyes were as wide as saucers and for a moment, everything just slipped away. There was just him, Joe and Ollie in the whole world.

"Really? Can I have an ice cream too?"

Chris laughed. "Let's just leave Mum in peace for a few hours. We can decide about ice creams later."

Ollie scooped up some more egg, shovelled it in and dropped his spoon onto the table. "I'm ready."

*

They spent the next few hours on the beach at Sennen. The rain stopped for brief periods and occasionally the sun tried to force its way through the heavy, grey cloud. The attempts were unsuccessful though and the day remained of the variety best spent indoors. However, watching Ollie clambering over the rocks was captivating. Listening to his excited voice rise above the turning waves was worth it. It was worth all of it.

There was already a collection of clothes for Ollie at Joe's. Some, particularly the Wellington boots, were too small, but Ollie didn't mind cramming his feet into them if it meant a day at the beach.

Joe and Chris walked side by side. The low tide enabled them to walk straight through to Gwynver beach. Chris had always loved Gwynver, not just because the surf was higher, more spectacular and dangerous but because he associated it with sitting beside Joe as a boy, listening to his stories about King Arthur and Guinevere. Those stories had inspired him to start writing his own tales about King Arthur. He'd left out the part about Arthur and Guinevere kissing on the beach because that was just yucky but the desire to write stories had stayed with him ever since. He had an idea Joe had made them up as a distraction, for both of them.

In the distance and out at sea, the rock formation known as The Brisons were being battered by the Atlantic Ocean, throwing white spray high into the air. The headland of Cape Cornwall was just visible too but just around the next headland, hidden away, was Hawk's Cove. It was a place that had seen two deaths in Chris's lifetime. One of them just yesterday. Chris could almost feel its presence as they walked closer.

"The tide will be coming in soon, we ought to turn around and walk back to Sennen." It was as if Joe didn't want to get too close either.

"Good thinking." He looked across the sand at Ollie who was clambering over a group of black rocks. His new red bucket was swinging from his hand like a lantern. He was safe there, well away from the tumbling waves. To get to Ollie, the sea would have to come through him first.

"Ollie! We're going back this way now." He pointed back toward Sennen.

Ollie put his thumb up and clambered back the other way. In the summer, if the weather was good, Gwynver was packed. There was a long, steep walk down from the car park but it was always worth it. It was too much for Joe to manage now but he was happy to walk back along the sand to Sennen where the car park was more accessible.

"How's that hand of yours?"

Chris held it up. The skin really didn't fit anymore; it was stretched and shiny where it was pulled over the swollen knuckles. Bruises were starting to bloom on his fingers. He tried to wiggle them and stopped immediately with a wince.

"Sore," he replied. It was a good job he didn't have any writing deadlines to meet.

"Looks like you might have broken something there."

"It was worth it."

"Yes. Yes it was."

Chris stopped and touched Joe on the arm. "We don't have to mention it to Lou though."

Joe held his own bunched fist up and pointed at a long scar which ran from knuckle to wrist. It was an old one that Chris had always assumed came from his fishing or mining days. "Just like she doesn't need to know where this came from."

"Jimmy Upson?"

Joe nodded and they carried on walking.

Having Ollie around had softened the blow of losing Pat but Joe was still not himself. There was something missing from his eyes. The spark that made a ninety-one year old man look and act like a fifty year old had gone. Every time Chris looked at him now, he could see it had diminished. Life had chewed off one more piece of him. How many more pieces were left? That was a question none of them wanted to ask.

He owed it to the man to tell him why Lou and Ollie were here, even more so because he didn't expect or need to be told. But to voice it would seem, and feel, like madness. Besides, he needed to have a conversation with Lou before he said anything.

"You said you saw Lizzy last night. Over in the field."

"That I did and she's up there now, looking down on us." He pointed upwards, at the top of the cliff but he did so without turning his head.

Chris looked up but there was nothing and nobody. He hadn't expected there to be.

"You normally wave or something."

Joe stopped. "Are you making fun of me?"

"No, of course not." In the pub, a couple of nights ago, he thought Joe might be teasing him, but now the roles were reversed. "I wouldn't do that, Granddad. Not now."

Joe turned and carried on walking but the slight tilt of his head toward the top of the cliff hadn't gone unnoticed.

"It doesn't seem right, not now she's following me about like this. Never seen the likes before. Only ever seen her up in the cemetery looking after your dad, that's the only place I've ever seen her. I don't know what she wants but I can't say as I like it."

Chris didn't like it either. He didn't like it one bit. He looked up at the clifftop again but all he could see were the leaden skies above it.

Joe changed the subject. "Let's go and find that ice cream for the boy."

*

By the time they arrived home, it was mid-afternoon. Ollie had eaten an ice cream as his first course, then they stopped for pasties and took them down to the cape. They'd eaten them in the car because of the rain but the enclosed space only heightened the delicious smell. Joe sat in the back seat with Ollie and pointed out the various landmarks that were still visible. He'd heard them all before but he was now old enough to be able to fire questions back at Joe. They never stopped talking except to push warm pasty into their mouths.

Chris told Ollie to be quiet when they went home so he wouldn't wake Lou, but when they walked into the kitchen she was sitting at the table. She hadn't been up long though because her hair was still wet from a shower.

"Mum, come and see what I've caught!" Ollie ran straight over and grabbed her hand. She followed him to the back door, where Ollie had left his bucket just outside.

"There's some fish in there. Look!"

There might have been fish or there might not, but there was a lot of seaweed in the bucket and it was impossible to see much more than that.

"Oh yes," Lou said.

"I caught them all by myself too." He turned to Joe and Chris. "Didn't I?"

Both of them said, "Yes," in unison.

Ollie came back to the table looking very proud of himself. "Dad said we could play Risk this afternoon. I'll go and fetch it."

"Whoa there!" Lou closed the door. "You need a shower. Those clothes are covered in wet sand and your head is more sand than hair. Strip off and up you go."

Ollie sighed and dropped his shoulders. Seven and he was exhibiting signs of a teenage tantrum.

"After?" he asked.

"That would be lovely. We'll all play and you can thrash us all. Okay?" Lou sounded livelier than she had this morning but it could just be *The Ollie Effect.*

He was already discarding clothes all over the kitchen as he made his way to the stairs.

Lou followed him but just as she reached the stairs, she turned and gave them both two thumbs-up. There was even a trace of smile, of happy smile, in there. Chris felt like it too but it was probably just Ollie. His mood was infectious.

"She looked a bit better than she did this morning," Chris said.

"She did but everyone does with a smile on their face." Joe nudged him and Chris realised he too was smiling.

Within half an hour, Ollie came hurtling down the stairs. He was dressed in his Marvel Avengers pyjamas with a particularly aggressive-looking Incredible Hulk on the front.

"Mum said it was alright for me to have a pyjama day, what's left of it anyway." He stood at the bottom of the stairs, between the front room and the kitchen. "Can I get Risk now?" he asked.

"You know where it is," Joe replied.

The game would take two hours to finish and somewhere along the way Ollie would find himself with a extra piece or two that had just miraculously appeared.

Ollie flicked the light on and went into the front room. "Can we have a fire later too? I'll help Granddad, I can…" There was a terrible scream and both of them stood up immediately. Chris pushed his chair back and started running toward the front room, toward Ollie. Upstairs he could hear Lou's footsteps moving quickly across the floorboards.

"Ollie!" Chris called as he got to the stairs. He was aware of Lou coming down toward him and he could see Ollie in the corner of the room. He was lying crumpled on the floor.

"Mum!" he wailed.

Chris went in first but Ollie always called for Lou when he was hurt.

"My foot, my foot, my foot!" he repeated. Chris bent down and scooped him up. The pressure in his swollen fist sent a bolt of pain through his body but he ignored it.

"God, look at his foot!" Lou hissed. "Bring him upstairs to the bathroom."

Ollie was crying but it wasn't the hysterical sound he'd made last night.

"Put him there and bring me a clean towel." She indicated the toilet and Chris put him down gently. "Now lift your leg so Mum can see it properly."

Chris opened the boiler cupboard and grabbed a towel. "Is it deep?"

She took the towel and dabbed at the blood. "No, not deep but there's lots of cuts."

Chris moved to the side and took Ollie's hand. "Will I have to go to hospital?" he asked. He was still crying but not quite as hard.

"I don't think we need to worry about that, do we Mum?"

Lou shook her head. "Just get me another towel, would you?"

Chris let go of Ollie's hand and fetched another one. "Might not be surfing for a few days, big man."

Ollie started crying hard again and Lou shot him a fierce look.

"Not unless we get you one of those special rubber socks." Chris tried to rescue the situation.

Ollie stopped crying and looked up at him. "What? Like Jacob wears at swimming? He's got verrucas, you know."

"That's it, just like those. I'm sure we can find somewhere in Penzance that sells them. What do you reckon, Mum?"

Lou wiped away more blood, allowing Chris to see the damage. There were lots of shallow scratches and three or four deep cuts. Thankfully all but one had stopped bleeding. "We'll see how you are tomorrow, eh?"

"I'll be fine," Ollie wiped away his tears. "Can we play Risk now?"

Chris almost laughed. "We might need to put a bandage on it first. I'll go and find one."

Ollie's eyes lit up again. "I'll need a big one, Dad!"

Chris did laugh then and he could hear Ollie chatting away to Lou as he walked back downstairs. Joe was in the front room.

"How is he?" he asked.

Chris popped his head into the room. "Oh, I think he'll live. We just need a bandage. A big one too."

Joe turned away and looked at the floor. He waved his arm distractedly toward the kitchen. "In the cupboard next to the sink."

Chris took a step toward the kitchen and then turned back. Joe was still staring at the floor. "What is it? Glass?"

"What?" He turned and looked back at Chris. "Yes. Yes it's glass, but…"

Chris walked to him and stopped. On the floor, beside the dresser where the game was kept and the shelf where the photographs were on show, were splinters and shards of glass. It was like a minefield for bare feet. Ollie had walked straight into it.

Next to the glass were two frames. Their silver sides were twisted and warped as if they had collided with something. Joe reached over the glass and picked them out. They were both face-down but even before he turned them over, they both knew which photographs they were.

Joe brushed away the remaining fragments of glass wedged into the frame and passed one to Chris.

It was of him, Lou and Ollie at the cape two years ago. They hadn't just fallen from the shelf when Ollie had come in. Chris had dropped one the other night and it hadn't smashed. No, these had been thrown to the floor and stamped on; stamped on with real rage.

He looked from his own photograph to Joe's. Joe ran his finger over his son's face.

"My boy." His finger left a smear of blood over the picture.

Chapter 15

Ollie was in bed and Joe had gone to the pub. They'd all played Risk and eaten fish and chips for tea, but Chris found it difficult to show any enthusiasm for either. Lou had looked at him a few times. She put her hand over his when she could see those all-too-familiar signs that all was not right in the house of Chris.

He'd smiled back, as he had hundreds of times over the last year, but saw the same worried expression come back from her a hundred times before. They both knew things were still a very, very long way from being normal. Ollie had gone off to sleep quickly though with no mention of what happened during the previous night. Perhaps it had slipped away into the part of his mind that kept nightmares locked away. Perhaps.

In any case, just being there to give him a kiss as he went off to sleep had lightened Chris's mood a little.

"I feel like there's so much I need to say, Lou. I don't

know where to begin. I mean, last night…"

"No, not last night. Not yet."

He nodded. They were going to go there at some point tonight. They had to and if he was right, it would all come to that anyway. He poured them both a glass of Sauvignon Blanc and sat down at the table. There was no way he could face any more beer or cider.

"Well, I found out my dad was going to kill himself." There, that was a start. It felt like a terrible thing to say but it was the truth.

"What?"

"Joe had a note. Well, Mum actually found the note when we were down here on that holiday. She found it while I was out with him on that day."

Lou reached across and took his hand. "Oh God, Chris. Oh God. When did Joe tell you?"

"The day I got down here. We had this huge talk and everything came out. All of it." He pointed at the drawer. "He'd kept it in there."

Lou didn't look, she kept her eyes on him. "And… who… shit, I'm sorry, I don't really know what to say."

"And neither did I. There were a lot of tears though, from both of us."

Lou shook her head and let out a long breath. "And your mum? Why didn't either of them mention it? Not at the time, I can understand that but to leave it this long, it's… well I'm not sure what it is."

"Look, I don't blame either of them. What do you do? Let a boy carry on believing his dad was a hero and that he died saving you, and in doing that give him a huge sack of guilt to lug around for the rest of his life?" He paused and looked to the ceiling. "Or you tell him the truth and say that his dad, who he thought was a hero, was going to leave him? Permanently. Either way, you're screwed."

"But I've seen what this has done to you. I've listened to you, Chris. I've seen the look on your face when you've been thinking about it. This *has* screwed you up. Completely and utterly. You are a fuck-up."

"Oh cheers, thanks for that." He tried to laugh but it didn't sound right, even to him.

She squeezed his hand. "You know it's true. That's why you're here. That's why I chucked you out."

"You didn't chuck me out. I left of my own accord."

"Yeah, right. Well if you hadn't gone, I had a crowbar with your name on it."

"And I would've deserved it. You're right, I am messed up but I'm still here and I'm fighting."

She let go of his hand and took a drink. "And tell me I'll never find a note from you, Chris."

"What?"

"Just tell me."

"Come on, Lou. I'm coming back here, I'm on my way back to you. And to Ollie. There won't be any notes. Okay?"

Lou nodded. "Better not be or I'll come for you."

She took his hand again. "So, how do you feel about him? How do you feel about him now?"

"I don't know, and that's the honest answer, Lou, I don't know. Granddad said Dad had always felt guilty about killing his own mum…"

"Sorry?"

Chris rubbed his face. "I'm sorry, that's something else I should've mentioned. Dad's mum, Grandma, died giving birth to him. Saying he killed her, that's wrong, but you get the picture."

Lou raised both hands and slapped her cheeks. "Poor Joe. Poor, poor Joe."

"Well, Joe thinks Dad was carrying that around with him. I'll have to speak to Mum at some point and find out but if he was anything like I've been, I've probably been wrong about her too." He took a long drink. "What a mess. You married into a right lot, didn't you?"

"You're not kidding."

"Oh, you're all heart."

"I am if it comes to my little boy, Chris. That's all that matters. He needs a dad, but he doesn't need one who scares the shit out of him, or just isn't there. He needs a dad." She looked out of the window into the darkness. Chris knew she loved how dark it got here, how many stars there were and how big the moon always was.

"I know that. I know what he needs. I know it because I didn't have it. Look at me, Lou."

She turned away from the window.

"When they found Pat, I was there. I was at Hawk's Cove with Joe, standing right by his side. I felt sick to my guts and it took every ounce of strength I had just to get out of the car and look down there again. You know how I feel about that place. I've never been back, not once have I even considered it, but I was there yesterday. I was there. And that means everything. I could do it. I can do it again and I can keep doing it. I'm not explaining myself very well, I know I'm not, but…"

"I know what you're saying. I understand what it is you're trying to do. You're trying to prove to yourself that you're dealing with it. I can see that."

They sat in silence for a minute or two and both drank some more wine.

"Pat told me some stories about Dad, some Joe doesn't know and it's best he never knows." He could feel a smile start to grow but it was stopped dead in its tracks as soon as the natural flow of his thoughts took him to Pendeen. Took him to her.

There was a silence again and this time it felt awkward. It felt that way because both of them knew what was coming next. What must come next. He could tell her about Pendeen, and about the look on Pat's face. He could tell her that as he looked into the place where her eyes should have been, all he saw was despair, utter despair, and he would have stepped over the precipice sooner than look into that blackness any longer. He could describe the anger he felt radiating off her too. The strength of it was so perfect and flawless as to be nauseating. He could say all of that and Lou would sit there and listen to it.

But would he be left with the blank look of denial and incomprehension that Pat had given him? Would all that he had said before about getting better and stronger slide into the sea, disappear along with Pat's blood?

"What did you see, Lou? What did you see in Ollie's room last night?"

She didn't respond immediately but he could see her jaw muscles working through her cheeks. Was she going to do what Pat did? Was she going down that road? Because if she did, well that might just put him back to where he was on the night he'd driven down here. On that night he'd had one foot inside the psychiatric ward.

She looked at him, opened her mouth, shut it again and looked away.

He reached over and gently guided her face toward his. "You've kept this family together for God knows how long now. You've protected Ollie and you've tried your best to help me. Now it's my turn to listen to you. We're in this together now."

She wanted to speak, he could see it in her eyes, but once she voiced what she'd seen there was no taking it back.

"It was the worst thing I've ever seen. It was… it was vile."

Chris nodded, he didn't want to say anything, lest it interrupt her flow.

"It… I mean *she,* and it was a she, Chris… was standing over Ollie. Standing over him like she owned him or something. I thank God he was under the covers because if he'd seen her, if he'd looked into those eyes and saw what I saw then he'd still be screaming now." She stopped and stared into space. "Holes. Great, black endless holes and I felt myself being drawn into them. I could feel endless pain in there. I could feel it, actually feel it and I was slipping closer and closer toward it and what was at the end was relief, but it was death too, it was death. Blackness, Chris. Just blackness, eternal, excruciating pain."

She turned her head and Chris could see the tears in her eyes.

"I almost felt sorry for her but she wanted our boy. I could feel it when she saw me. It was radiating off her like a beacon, only it wasn't light, it was darkness. And I knew if Ollie saw her, he would be gone. He would slip into those holes and never come out."

She stopped, wiped her eyes and drained her glass.

"It's madness, absolute madness, I know it is and I know what you'll say. You'll say that I'm under stress and Ollie made it up to bring you home but it…"

"I've seen her too. I saw her when I was seven, Lou. I saw her when my dad died and I saw her two nights ago at Pendeen with Pat."

"What?" Lou was the only person who had never questioned her existence, but her eyes were filled with confusion. "You think it's the same woman? Chris, that's ridiculous. It doesn't make sense. How can…"

"So what we've seen, what we've both seen, is perfectly logical is it? To see and feel exactly the same thing isn't ridiculous, it isn't part of a nightmare. It's the truth and it's happening to us, all three of us."

Lou crossed her arms, rested them on the table and buried her face in them. Her voice was muffled but it was still audible. "I don't understand. I don't understand any of it and every time I close my eyes, even just to blink, I can see her. I can see those long fingers running like water toward Ollie." She lifted her head and finished her wine. "What about Joe? Does he know about her? Have you told him about last night, or about Pendeen?"

"I haven't said a word. How can I?" He shrugged. "I know Pat saw her too though and I'm pretty sure he'd seen her before. He wouldn't listen and we got into a fight about it." He stopped and reached for the bottle. There was only a little bit left but Lou covered the top of her glass. "But he'd gone by the next morning. He was already down at Hawk's."

"Is that why your hand's like that?"

Chris looked at it and nodded. He'd been given an easy out and he was taking it.

"Do you think we should talk to Joe about it? Would he understand, do you think?" Lou was not interested in the hand, which was good.

Chris shook his head. "I don't know. He's surprised me this week."

"With what?"

"He believes in ghosts, for one thing. And he keeps talking about Lizzy. Reckons he's seen her on the lane up there and then down at Gwynver. But this, this is different."

Lou nodded. "Well, you know him better than anyone so I'll leave that decision to you. We're safe here though, that's the main thing."

Chris glanced toward the front room.

"Chris? We're safe here, aren't we?"

He smiled and took her hand again. "Sorry, I was miles away. Yes, of course we are. This is the safest place in the world." And it had always felt that way since he was a little boy. But the photographs, they were concerning.

*

Whenever they came to stay at Joe's, Lou always insisted on having the bedroom window open when they went to bed. She loved to hear the distant crash of waves rumble into the room as she fell asleep. Tonight she hadn't mentioned it and Chris wasn't going to mention it either.

She lay against him with her head on his chest and when her twitching body woke her, she rolled over. Chris lay there staring at the dark space above his head. He hadn't slept much the night before so was exhausted, but everything was spinning around and around and around in his head like a carousel. As each thought appeared, he was just getting to grips with it before it spun away and was replaced by something else. It happened over and over again and it was making him dizzy. Were they safe? Was Ollie really safe here? What was this all about? And why was this… woman doing this? Hadn't she done enough?

At some point he heard Joe come in. He listened to each of his footsteps as he climbed the stairs. Joe didn't need this brought to his door. He'd been through too much and lost too much for something else to try and knock him down.

He lay there and as the thought carousel revolved in seeming perpetuity, his eyes grew heavy and he allowed them to close. If they weren't safe here, they weren't safe anywhere.

*

He was aware of a voice in the house. It was Joe's voice and he was upset or angry, or maybe both but he needed help.

Chris lay there and waited. Had it been a dream? His eyes started to close again. Just a dream, that was all.

"No." It was a growl, the sound of someone trying not to make too much noise.

He rubbed his eyes and slid his feet over the side of the bed. He listened again but all he could hear was the sound of Lou's heavy breathing. Maybe Joe was having a nightmare. He sighed, now he was awake he needed to go to the toilet anyway; too much wine just before bedtime was responsible.

He pushed the screen on his phone. It was just after one. He couldn't have been asleep for very long. He padded quietly across the room and opened the door. It creaked a little but not enough to wake anyone.

"No, no, no." This time it was louder but not full volume. Chris stood at the top of the stairs. It was Joe's voice but it hadn't come from his room, it had come from downstairs. Either from the kitchen or the front room.

He reached around the bedroom door and grabbed the dressing gown. Maybe it was just a visitor, one of his pals from the pub, but it didn't sound right. Anyway, he'd heard Joe come up to bed.

He pulled the dressing gown cord and stepped quietly down the stairs. He'd never known Joe to sleepwalk before but there was always a first.

He stopped at the bottom of the stairs and looked into the kitchen. It was dark, no sign or shape of humanity in there. He turned the other way. Joe was silhouetted in profile against the window. He was staring at the spaces where the two picture frames had been. Both frames were now in the bin but the pictures had been laid flat, ready for new ones.

"You can't just come in here like this. I won't have it."

Chris opened his mouth to apologise before he realised Joe wasn't talking to him.

"It's my house. Go back to where you belong." Joe's voice was shaking as he spoke.

Chris wanted to go in and take Joe back upstairs. He was sleepwalking and dreaming but wasn't there a rule about not waking sleepwalkers? Something in the back of his mind told him that it was a bad idea to wake him up.

"Please, Lizzy, please just take him."

Chris went cold.

"He shouldn't be here. Neither of you should. Please."

Despite his intentions, Chris took a step inside the room. He had to be sure there was nobody else there and there wasn't. Joe was all alone but he hadn't noticed Chris.

"I don't know what you want, son. I don't know what you want but you should be somewhere else now. You both should be." Joe's voice cracked completely and he fell against the dresser, sobbing.

Chris jumped forward. "Granddad." He tried to whisper but he knew he was almost shouting. He grabbed Joe's arm and as he did so, he felt the hairs on the back of neck bristle. He shivered involuntarily.

Joe grabbed Chris's arm and pulled him close. "They're here, they're both here," he whispered.

Chris could see streaks of tears rolling down his cheeks. "Who's here? Who is it?" He was sure Joe wasn't sleepwalking now.

He turned his head and looked Chris straight in the eye. "Lizzy and Jack. They're here, inside my house. They're…" His voice trailed off and he slumped against Chris.

The big, baggy jumpers and the over-sized dressing gown couldn't disguise how thin Joe had become. Chris could feel every bone in his body through his ancient pyjamas. He didn't want to turn around and look into the space where Joe had been looking a moment ago in case he saw something, or someone, he didn't want to.

"Come on, Granddad, I'll help you back upstairs," he whispered.

Chris didn't exactly drag him but it wasn't far off. Joe's legs moved but his feet were slow to follow suit. Chris couldn't have done this five years ago, or maybe even two, but Joe had lost so much weight that it almost made Chris cry to think about it.

He was still fit though. He was still a vital man who could walk miles and miles in a day without ache or pain.

"Joe, you're going to need to help me up the stairs, okay?"

Joe went rigid against him. Chris could tell by the hot breath on his cheek that Joe had turned to face him. If he'd turned too, their noses would touch.

"Did you see him, did you see your dad?"

A chill went through him. "I didn't see anyone. You need to help me."

Joe gently pushed him away. "They should be

somewhere else. They shouldn't be in this house."

Joe started up the stairs on his own but Chris followed closely behind. As they reached the top, Joe turned toward his room.

"Granddad, I think I... no, I need to talk to you." He tried to whisper but it was louder than that. Something was happening now and whether or not it was all connected, Chris owed it to the man. He owed the man who'd acted like a father for the last thirty-three years to be straight with him. He owed him more than that but the rest he could never hope to repay.

Joe turned. "And I need to speak to you." He walked into his bedroom and started to close the door.

"And I think your dad will be listening." He closed the door completely, leaving Chris on the landing.

What did that mean? He stood still and stared at Joe's door, then turned and went back to his own room. Lou had changed position but she was still breathing heavily.

What on earth did Joe mean?

Chapter 16

"I wonder if you and Mum might like to spend some time at Land's End this morning? Lollipop's got some spends for you?"

Chris had asked Lou if she could give him time to speak to Joe alone. He hadn't mentioned the incident involving Joe in the night, but he had told her he was going to talk about *her*.

Ollie looked up from his egg. Once again there was butter on his cheeks and yolk on his chin. Gerald the giraffe was on the table next to him.

"And can I buy something made of plastic? Or one of those foam swords again?"

Joe put a twenty pound note on the table. "You can buy whatever you want as long as you buy your mum an ice cream."

Ollie grabbed the money and gave it to Lou. He hadn't wet the bed and he hadn't woken up at all in the night, so both of them looked a hundred times better than they had at the same time yesterday.

"You know what this means, Dad?"

"I've got a vague idea." Chris sounded better than he felt.

"If I get one of those foam swords, you'll never be safe again."

They all laughed, even Joe who looked like he'd aged ten years overnight. Chris had slept on and off for most of the night and been awake completely since four o'clock. At no time had he heard Joe get up and go for his walk. He had a feeling it was a very long time since the old boy hadn't taken that morning ritual.

"Are we going then?" Ollie finished his apple juice and stood up. His foot was bandaged but there were no traces of blood seeping through and he had hardly limped on the way down the stairs.

"You might need to get dressed first." Lou stood up and ushered him away.

"I'll put the kettle on then." Chris flicked the switch. "Will we need this?" He reached into the cupboard and grabbed the bottle of Bushmills.

Joe shook his head. "Lizzy won't like it." He tilted his head toward the stairs. "She won't leave, neither of them will."

Chris closed the cupboard door. "Granddad, please." Things were bad enough without hearing that. "Ollie might hear."

"Better than seeing," Joe replied.

Ollie and Lou had gone off for the day. While he'd been getting dressed, Ollie grew reluctant to leave but Chris had promised him he would be right here when he got back. He could even hit him over the head with the sword if he wanted to. Ollie had made them all stand in a circle, put their hands on top of each other's and promise they would always be together. None of them had complained about doing it.

Joe and Chris sat at the table facing each other, where it seemed they had almost entirely spent the last few days.

"I need to go first, Granddad. I need to say it out loud before I think myself out of it."

Joe just nodded. He looked like he wanted to get something off his chest before it suffocated him too.

"The woman, the woman down at the cove on the day Dad drowned, I did see her. I know I saw her because I've seen her since." He waited for a reaction. A voice of dissent, just as there had always been, or a widening of the eyes to indicate shock, but there was nothing. Not even a flicker. It disarmed Chris slightly but he carried on.

"I think I saw her up at the cemetery on the day we went to visit Dad, but I *know* I saw her at Pendeen when I was with Pat. There's no question about that. I'm pretty sure Pat saw her too." Now it was out there and he was talking about it, it didn't sound quite as bad as it had done in his head.

"Only, she doesn't look the same now. Something's changed, something… She's gone *lower* if that makes sense? Lower and darker, like the shadows are holding onto her. I don't know, it sounds ridiculous, like a dodgy film script. I don't know how to explain it."

He looked at Joe again but the man was impassive.

"Granddad?"

"I'm listening. You just keep talking and get it all off your chest. And then I'll say my piece."

"You remember I told you, Mum and the police about her eyes? About how they weren't there and how they made me feel? Well now it's still the same, *she's* still the same as that, only worse somehow." He paused and took a deep breath. "There's that creature in mythology – the Medusa who turns people to stone. Well she's like that but her eyes, or where her eyes should be, strip you back, right back and leave you with nothing. Life, happiness, love, willpower, it's all gone in an instant. So all that's left is sadness and grief. Overwhelming grief. The same grief I felt after that day at Hawk's."

He stopped again and tapped his forehead. "It's all in here anyway. All of it. She just flicks a switch and it all comes to the surface. Boom! And you don't just want to die, you want her to help you there."

He slapped his forehead.

"Jesus Christ, this is madness, absolute madness. I can't believe I'm thinking these things, let alone saying them."

He stood up and walked around the table. He'd questioned his sanity so many times over the last thirty-three years, it was second nature, but this wasn't just his own sanity he had to consider now. He sat back down.

"And the worst thing about all of this is Ollie."

For the first time, he saw a flicker of emotion from Joe and was pleased.

"Ollie's seen her too. I don't know how many times for sure, but at least once. That's why they're here, Granddad. The night before they got here, she was there in his room, trying to pull back the covers, trying to look into his eyes and do what she's trying to do to me. She wants us both, I don't know why but she wants us. She won't have my son though. She won't touch him, I can tell you that."

Anger started to rise to the surface. It wasn't as powerful as he'd felt with Tallack but it was there.

"Nobody is touching either of you." Joe spoke loudly and with the rock-steady tone it had always had.

"I went to speak to Pat, you know. That's where I was coming from on the morning they found him. We had a fight about her. He wouldn't listen to me. I didn't know what was wrong with him then but that's why he was down there on that slipway. *She's* the reason his blood was all over the slipway."

He drew a deep breath and tried to clench his broken fist. The pain spurred him on. "He'd seen her before, I know he had. I think that was just the last straw. *She* killed him." Chris threw his head back. He was babbling and it all made sense to him, but Joe had barely said anything. "What the f…" Joe hated swearing. "What the hell is going on? I'm going down the same route as Dad."

Joe stood up and walked into the front room.

Chris felt better for unloading like that. He'd done it countless times over the years, although never about anything quite so disturbing or absurd-sounding.

Joe came back in and put a file on the table. "You're right about Pat." He pushed it over to Chris. "Have a look in there."

The file was a simple A4 docket. It was a faded green colour and he recognised it straight away. It had been his when he was a little boy. Joe had scribbled black ink over the top of the name, *Christopher*, but it was still just visible. He'd kept his stories in there. All of them ripped carefully from his little notebook.

He lifted the flap. What he found weren't the stories of a little boy, perfecting an art he would come to rely on in later life. No, what he found were the disturbed rants of a man who was trying his hardest not to end up on the slipway at Hawk's Cove with his wrists gouged down to the bone.

He pulled the wad of paper out. It was four inches thick and made from paper of varying sizes. As the bundle came clear of the docket, some of the smaller pieces fluttered down to the floor. He ignored them because it was the image on the top sheet which caught his attention.

On the page, in black ink, were two large circles side by side. They had been drawn over and over again. As Chris picked it up, he could feel the indentations made by the heavy hand that had made them.

"All Pat's work. All of it."

Inside the two circles, Pat had drawn two crosses. Again they had been overwritten so many times that at the very tips, the pen had punctured the paper.

Chris put it to one side and looked up. "There are so many."

"And the first few I just threw in the bin."

Chris leafed through them quickly. They were mostly of the same two circles scrawled heavily into the page, some with crosses, some without but on others Pat had written something.

"How did you get these?" Chris asked.

"He posted them through the door. Sometimes I'd go for weeks without getting any, and then there would be weeks where they would come every day."

Chris read one aloud. "Don't look, she's coming." The words were written beneath the circles again, but this time they were filled in.

"He had seen her before." He held the paper up like a trophy. "I knew he had."

Joe nodded. "And then there's the notes. The suicide notes." He reached across and pushed the papers to one side. At the bottom was a collection of carefully folded sheets. They were different.

"Saying the same thing over and over and over."

Chris unfolded one. "I'm sorry, I'm sorry, I'm sorry, I'm sorry, I'm sorry…" The whole page was filled with the same thing. He opened the next one and two more after that. Each one was filled with exactly the same thing. Over and over again.

"The first time I got one of those was the day after you'd gone back up north with your mum. About a week after we put Jack in the ground. I knew what it was and I knew what was in his mind. I spent the day down the road there at Hawk's waiting for him. I waited until it was so dark I couldn't see the path anymore; just me, the sea and the rocks. I thought I saw your dad a time or two then, floating in on the tide and banging his head in the rocks. But Pat didn't come."

Joe scratched his head. "I waited the next week too, when I got another. And the time after that. I must have spent about two weeks waiting for that great big idiot to come down there and do something stupid to himself. The first time he sent a note and I didn't go down there, I walked up and down the kitchen all day until my feet bled. Eventually, after a few years, I realised he wasn't going to do it, but by then he was drinking like a fish. He was probably too drunk to hold a knife most of the time, let alone…" He stopped there. Pat hadn't been too drunk two days ago.

Chris held two sheets of paper side by side. One with the circles drawn on and one with his apology.

"What was he sorry about, Granddad?" He put the pages down.

Joe bit his lip. "What were *we* sorry about. That's a better question."

Some of it I can tell you first hand, I was there, but the rest, I can only repeat what the boys told me. I didn't want to tell you this. For all the world I never wanted to tell you, but I won't see this go on and I won't see anybody else's body down there." He hooked a thumb over his shoulder toward Hawk's Cove.

"Little Ollie…" Joe stopped and coughed. "He looks just like Jack did at that age. His face is burned into my brain and no matter how long passes, he's there. I won't see you or your little boy suffer for what we did."

"Joe, you're starting to scare me here and I'm already… If this isn't something we need to know now then…"

"You need to know now. It's all connected. All of it. And you and Ollie are in the middle."

Chapter 17

August 1969

"Slow down there, Jackie-boy. I nearly spilled the beer."

Jack took his foot off the accelerator just a touch and then hammered it down to the metal. Pat lurched forward, spilling more beer down his shirt.

"You did that on purpose!"

"Yep."

They were out on the road again. They had a tank full of petrol, a packet of Embassy and a bottle of Dad's home brew in the back. All courtesy of a stint on the pots.

"Reckon Joe will notice his beer stash has gone down?" Pat asked.

"He won't mind." And Dad wouldn't mind. Not as long as Jack was up and fit for five in the morning. He pulled up to a junction. It was left to St Ives or right to Penzance.

"Where we going then?" Pat pushed two cigarettes into his mouth and lit them both. He handed one to Jack.

It was mid-September and the summer had been long and hot. Long, hot and hard work for the pair of them. Joe paid them well for working the pots but the money just went straight into the tank of the Hillman Minx.

"I'm not going to go and sit in the park again, Pat. I'm not going to wait for Susie Curnow to flash her tits at me."

"St Ives then, let's take a nice slow drive up there."

Jack wound down the window and then pushed the car into first gear. He accelerated hard out of the junction, sending a cloud of cigarette smoke into his eyes and ash into his lap. He wasn't that keen on smoking, neither of them was, but Pat thought they looked like film stars when they smoked and that was a good enough reason. He preferred the smell of the sea and of the land, particularly when the sun had been on them all day and cooked them up into a rich, heady brew.

He intended making the most of the last few days here, especially of the time with Pat. Once he went up to Exeter they probably wouldn't see each other until Christmas. It'd be tough but it's what Mum would've wanted so he was happy to go. Besides, Dad would look after Pat. He'd been doing it for the last fifteen years so Pat would be okay. Maybe he'd get off his arse and do his share of work when Jack had gone.

"So, you're going to have to get used to some early mornings when I'm gone. You'll have to cut back on this." He pointed at the glass bottle in Pat's hand. The beer inside looked dangerous.

"Sooner that than the pit." Pat took a drink and offered it across.

Jack took a quick drink and passed it back. "He won't let you go down there. I know he goes on about it but it's just a threat. He wouldn't let you."

"Your dad is like a god," Pat announced and blew smoke out of the window. "He's better than that actually. You don't have to pray to Joe, you just have to bring his pots in."

They both laughed.

"You better come up and see me." Jack knew every bend on the road and he turned hard left into one, making the back end of the Minx twitch.

"Course I will but we've got the rest of the summer yet so don't talk about it."

He knew Pat was worried about him going away. They'd been inseparable for the last fifteen years and now that their contact was coming to a temporary pause, Pat wouldn't talk about it. He probably didn't want to think about it either.

He was right though, they did have the rest of the summer, the last couple of days anyway. Jack pushed down hard on the accelerator. Over Pat's shoulder, jagged shards of amber bounced off the sea as the sun set on the last few days of the season. You could never leave a place like this, not for long.

Pat switched the radio on and The Stones were singing about Honky Tonk Women. He joined in with Mick Jagger and it was a toss-up as to who was the loudest. Pat liked music as long as he could shout along with it and The Stones were good for that. Mortimer's Garage had fitted the radio at the cost of a week's work with Joe but it was worth every penny.

"What's the fastest we've got out of her?" Pat turned the radio down as Jagger rolled into Thunderclap Newman.

"I don't know. Sixty maybe, seventy tops. She doesn't like it much faster than that."

Pat tapped the dashboard "Poor baby. Let's see how fast you can really go." He reached over and squeezed Jack's leg, just above the knee.

His leg jerked off the pedal causing them to lurch violently. The car jerked to the left, nearly sending them into the dry stone wall.

"Shit!" Jack shouted and straightened the car. He turned his head. "You're such a ... "

Pat's eyes widened and his jaw dropped. "Jack, watch out!"

Jack turned back to the road and in the same instant, he slammed his foot down on the brake and cranked the steering wheel as far to the right as it would go. A blurred vision of a scared but pretty face was framed in the dying light.

The back end of the Minx slid out to the left and for a split-second threatened to overtake the front end. Jack released the brake and then quickly stepped on it again bringing the car to an untidy halt across the middle of the road. The front end was partially in the hedge bottom, but at least it was greenery not stone.

He jumped out and ran the few steps toward the girl. "What the fuck are you doing walking in the middle of the road?"

"As good a place as any." She was prettier than his first fleeting glimpse suggested. Her long brown hair fell over her shoulders and onto her backpack. In that light she looked like Raquel Welch. He could smell Juicy Fruit chewing gum on her breath.

"Well you nearly got us all killed." It felt like his heart was beating a thousand times a minute. He looked back at the car. Pat was still climbing out.

She shrugged. "Sorry, I suppose." She was continually touching a silver pendant which hung around her neck. She turned it over and over in her fingers.

"Hey, there's no need for shouting. We can sort this. Take it easy Jackie-boy." *Pat strolled over like a film star. He was a good three inches taller than Jack and broader at the shoulders. He thought he looked like a young John Wayne. It was a shame nobody else did.*

"Where you guys heading?" *she asked.*

"Wherever you want us to be," *Pat drawled and tipped an imaginary hat.*

Jack sighed. "We're in Cornwall, Pat, not California."

"I've got some pot?" *The girl offered it like it was currency.*

"Well I'm Pat and this is Jack and that car over there is at your disposal."

"And I'm Carol." *She held her hand out to each of them in turn.* "If you're going to St Ives I'd love a ride. We can smoke a joint on the way?" *She hopped from foot to foot like she was agitated. It was unnerving.*

Neither of them had ever smoked pot before. "It's your lucky night, Carol." *Pat led her to the car. As he passed, he whispered to Jack,* "And mine too I reckon." *In a louder voice he told Carol*

"I'll ride in the back with you and we can have that smoke."

Jack watched them climb into the car. Pat had a way about him that girls seemed to find attractive. He, on the other hand, had struggled since the whole Susie Curnow experience. It had scarred him in more ways than one.

"Come on, mate," *Pat shouted out of the rear window. A cloud of smoke was already gathering about his head like a pillow. Jack loved the guy like a brother but sometimes he wished he would just take things a bit slower.*

He strolled slowly over and climbed into the front seat. "I feel like a chauffeur."

"St Ives please, James, and my friend Carol here would like to take a look at the lighthouse on the way so she can smoke this here marijuana." Pat put on a fake posh accent and Carol laughed like she was already stoned. She probably was.

Jack pulled off the main road and drove down the track toward the lighthouse. They occasionally brought girls up here. Or rather Pat brought them. They were usually girls they'd met at one of the dances in the surrounding villages. The night typically ended with Pat taking the girl for a 'walk' down by the clifftop while he sat in the car and tried to think of something interesting to say to the other one. It was usually a blessed relief to see Pat come back up the slope fifteen minutes later, tucking his shirt in and combing his hair. Sometimes it was longer and sometimes the 'walks' were shorter but Pat usually tipped him a wink when he climbed back in the car.

Carol and Pat had barely drawn breath, they were talking so much. Pat could be a real charmer when he wanted to.

"You like that necklace don't you?" Pat asked.

"Why d'you ask?

Jack looked in the mirror. She was still twisting it between her fingers.

"You just haven't left it alone. What is it?" Pat reached over and tried to touch it but she slapped his hand before he got close. It made Jack smile. He wasn't going to have it all his own way with her.

"Don't touch it." Her words were slightly slurred but her voice carried a threat.

Pat withdrew his hand and put it in his lap. "Sorry, miss. I didn't mean to do nothing wrong. I just saw something pretty and I wanted to touch it." He tried his American drawl routine again.

"We'll see about that." Her tone had softened again. She had boundaries and one of them was the pendant. Pat would probably try to test the other boundaries later.

The tyres crunched over the gravel and Jack brought the car to a stop. The lighthouse keeper wouldn't bother them if they didn't bother him, and it was clear from how much kissing was going on in the back that it wasn't going to be an issue.

Jack coughed loudly and caught Pat's eye in the mirror. "Be nice if you could show Carol the view from down there." He didn't want to sit here and listen to them going at it all night.

Pat winked back and turned to Carol. "Bring that joint and I'll show you the constellations." He was already out of the car and running around the other side to open the door for her.

Carol climbed out of the car as if she were scaling a mountain. As they passed, she leaned through the window and kissed Jack's cheek. "You look like Steve McQueen."

It was the best thing he'd ever heard. Their mouths were close enough for him to feel her breath on his lips. He could smell Juicy Fruit but he could also smell pot, and lots of it. She was stoned, definitely. Drunk, possibly. She wobbled off and took Pat's outstretched hand.

"Pat! Just come here for a sec," he shouted.

Pat kissed Carol for an age and walked slowly back. "What?"

"She's stoned, man. Absolutely out of it. She hasn't got a clue what's going on. We should just take her to St Ives and leave her there. She's…"

Pat interrupted. "She knows what she's doing. She's a big girl and she can make her own decisions. I'll just show her the view and come right back up. Just chill out." He stretched across and turned the volume up on the radio. "Just listen to some tunes and we'll be back before you know it." He wandered off, doing some sort of ridiculous dance move.

Jack watched them go down the slope until they were out of view. He turned the radio off, lit a cigarette and opened the door. Nobody needed a radio here and you didn't need beer or drugs either. You just needed to tune in to the sound of the waves hitting the rocks. There weren't many better sounds than that.

At least he wouldn't have to worry about trying to be interesting or making small talk. He could just sit here, and listen to the ocean. Pat didn't know the first thing about constellations, but if he did then tonight would be a perfect one for showing off some knowledge. The sky was clear and the first few stars had come out in a sky that was turning from dark blue to black.

He stepped out of the car and inhaled. It was a rich smell, full of strength, full of beauty and full of danger. The lighthouse sent out its first beam of light into the encroaching darkness. Soon he wouldn't have this on his doorstep. He'd taken it for granted for so long that, now he was on the verge of losing it, he found an appreciation that had been lacking for most of his life. He'd come back though. As soon as the course had finished, he'd be back here; drinking beer with Pat, listening to him shout his *way through another verse of something by The Stones, and talking about how they were going to change the world.*

He flicked his cigarette onto the gravel and ground his foot down on it. Tomorrow was going to be the last time he would be on the pots for a while. He was pleased Pat wouldn't be there because he wanted it to be just his dad and him. They didn't say much while they were out collecting the pots but they were together, and they were together as working men. That was enough. That was worth a million exchanged words. He felt a smile grow across his face. After Pat and Carol had finished watching the stars, or whatever else they were doing, he was going to drop her off at St Ives and drive straight back to the village. He didn't want to be up late and he didn't want to feel drunk or tired in the morning. He wanted to remember tomorrow for the rest of his life.

He looked at his hands. There wouldn't be many other students with hands like these. The rough and weathered palms were a testament to how many years Dad had made him work for his upkeep. That wasn't where his future lay though. No way. He was going to write books; hundreds of them. He was going to write about Cornwall, about the mines and the miners, about the boats and the fishermen. He was going to put all the stories Dad had ever told him onto paper.

He'd go and visit Mum on Sunday before he went. Dad would take some violets as usual and they would stand there in silence and stare at the headstone. It wasn't true silence though because Jack would be talking to her, all the time he'd be talking to her inside his head. Dad did it too, he knew that because he'd seen his lips moving while they stood there.

He climbed back inside the car and closed his eyes. He was going to miss the sound of the waves more than anything else. But it wasn't permanent. He just had to keep telling himself that. Dad hadn't said much, he never did, but he was proud of him. He just had to picture the look on his face when the acceptance letter came through to know that. The image of his dad fighting back the tears was all he needed to see. "Your mum would be so proud," *he'd said and wrapped his arms around him. That was all he needed.*

"Come on, we're going."

He came back to the now with a start. He hadn't heard Pat climb into the car. He shuffled forward and rubbed his eyes. "Dropped off."

"Looks like it. Come on." *Pat tapped the dashboard.*

"Give me a moment." *He started the engine and looked over his shoulder.* "Where's Carol?"

"No idea."

"What?"

Pat turned in his seat. "Jack, I don't know where she went." *He emphasised each word and it came across as sarcasm.*

"Well you better look for her then." *He did the same.*

Pat turned away. "Fuck off."

"What?"

"I said fuck off. I'm not going out there to look for her."

Jack opened his car door. "I'll go…"

He felt Pat's hand on his arm. "I walked her to the path. She said she wanted to walk to St Ives by the light of the moon or some other hippy shit. I pointed her in the right direction and off she went. She'll be halfway there by now."

Jack turned and looked at his friend. Carol had probably spurned his advances, that was why he was so pissed off.

"She told you to get lost, didn't she?"

Pat pulled a face. "Maybe."

Jack laughed and closed the door. "Losing your touch a bit there, Patty?" He hated being called that.

"Just drive us home and shut your mouth."

He flicked the lights on. "Some of that path isn't safe. I'm not sure we should just leave her."

"She was adamant. She wouldn't be budged."

"Not even when you tried to cop a feel?"

Pat turned and this time Jack saw a flash of something that jarred him. He had a fight with Pat once and he'd seen it then. They both ended up with blackened eyes and bloody noses that day, but Jack had been lucky that Joe had been there to break it up.

"Just drive the fuck home."

Jack opened his mouth. If this was what pot did to someone, he wanted no part of it. He was going to say something sarcastic but the timing would have been all wrong. He revved the engine and reversed back along the path until he could turn.

They drove back to the village in silence and when Jack dropped him off, Pat said goodbye with a wave of his hand and nothing more. They might only have a few days of summer left but if it was going to be like this then it might be hard work. One thing was for sure, Pat was better on beer than he was on dope.

"Night, Pat," he whispered to himself and drove away.

What time was it? Jack switched the lamp on and looked at his watch. It wasn't even three o'clock. He rubbed his eyes and waited for whatever it was that had woken him up to happen again.

'Chink.' He knew what it was straight away. It was someone throwing a stone at his window and that someone would be Pat.

He opened the window, looked out and saw a dark shape in the garden beneath.

"It's me," Pat whispered.

"What do you want?" Had he come to apologise for his behaviour?

"I need to talk to you. Come down and open up."

"Pat, it'll wait for the morning. I've got be up in another hour or so. I'll see you tomorrow." He started to close the window.

"Jack! I need to talk to you." His voice was more than a whisper now. Was he still high?

"Shut up, you'll wake Dad. I'll come down." He closed the window and pulled on his jeans and t-shirt. He was too tired to be angry but that might change in the next ten minutes depending on what Pat said.

He crept down the stairs and opened the door. Before Pat said anything, Jack whispered "Just keep it down. Just say what you need to say and go." If this was an apology, which wasn't really needed, it would only take a few seconds.

Pat walked straight in but he didn't sit down. "We've got to go back. Get your keys and let's go."

"Back where? What are you on about? Pat, you're still high,

just go back to bed. I'll…"

Pat grabbed the neck of his t-shirt and pulled him forward. Their noses bumped together. "Pendeen, we need to get back to Pendeen and find her."

Jack pulled away. "Carol? I thought you said…"

"Forget that, just get your keys and take me there."

Tears started dribbling down Pat's cheeks. The only time he'd ever seen Pat cry was when the kids at school teased him about finding his dad asleep in the gutters around the village.

"Okay, okay." He tapped his pocket. The car keys were still in there. "Just give me a moment to put something on my feet."

This felt bad. It had felt bad to him when they were there last night but now with Pat crying, it felt like something terrible was about to happen. He drove slowly away from the house. Something inside told him he wouldn't be back for four, to take the pots out with his dad.

"You better not be fucking me around, Pat."

Pat was silent. He just stared at the road ahead.

They parked the car back up the road from the lighthouse at Pat's insistence. It only added to the feeling of dread that was building quickly in Jack's stomach. His guts felt like they did on the first bad day at sea with his dad.

A dew had formed on the grass bank and Pat half fell, half slid down it in his haste to get to the bottom. Jack followed but slower. There hadn't been a conversation on the way or when they got here, just a barked order from Pat to stop the car.

Pat waited at the bottom of the bank. "Come on!" he hissed.

About ten feet beyond Pat were the rusted remains of two fence posts. The wire fence had long since gone but the posts remained. They were a warning marker about what was below; jagged rocks and waves that would smash you to bits in seconds.

Pat turned around the perimeter wall of the lighthouse and disappeared. There was a patch of overgrown grass that he liked to roll around with girls in just around the other side. It was discreet, especially at night.

Jack stopped briefly at the bottom of the bank. The wind was whipping up and down below. It sounded as if someone was trying to break the cover off a bass drum. Pat's form was briefly illuminated by the flash of the lighthouse. He was standing like a statue staring at the ground, only his hair was moving in the wind.

Jack jogged toward him. "Pat, what is it?" He knew though, he knew what he was running toward.

Pat turned to him. His hair blew across his face and hid his expression. "I think she's dead."

Jack looked down. Carol was lying in the grass and her wide eyes flashed like beacons as the lighthouse beam hit her. He dropped down to his knees immediately and felt her neck. There was dried vomit on her cheek and throat but there was no pulse. He looked down at her body. Her short skirt was hitched up around her waist and he could see her knickers in the grass to the side.

He looked up. "Pat?"

Pat just stared down at her. He didn't move.

Jack stood up and grabbed him by his jacket collar. "Pat, what the fuck happened here? What did you do to her?" He looked down. "You told me she'd gone off on the path." The dread he'd been feeling had turned into gut-wrenching horror.

"We were going for it," Pat started, but gone was the assured, cocky man from last night. In his place was the little boy being teased in the playground.

"And she was going for it, full on and laughing, like she was really loving it. And then she started with this shaking and her whole body starts convulsing and she's choking and…" Pat was sobbing but he couldn't take his eyes off her.

"We need to take her to the hospital," Jack dropped down. "Help me put her pants on, for God's sake!" He touched her skin again and recoiled. She was cold and her skin felt hard somehow.

"We can't."

"What?" Jack was trying to pull her underwear back on. "Pat, help me!"

"We can't take her. The police will come and I'll go to prison. They'll say I forced her or something."

Jack stood up. "Pat, we need to get her to the hospital. You didn't do anything wrong. She took too much dope or something, I don't know. Just help me." He knelt down. The dew was coming through his jeans. It told him that this wasn't a dream, it wasn't a very bad dream, it was real.

"No, Jack. You're wrong. I know what'll happen. They'll have me Jack, they'll take me away and I'll never see you or Joe again." He turned away and looked at the sea. His voice was deadpan, as if he'd shut down.

"I might as well jump."

He started walking quickly toward the clifftop.

Jack jumped up and sprinted toward him. He rugby-tackled him about a metre away from the edge and rolled him away. A *flash of white water thirty metres below jagged across his vision as they both came close to going over.*

Jack was up in a second. He pinned Pat to the grass by kneeling on his arms. "You listen to me, you shithead, you're not going over the edge, not tonight." Pat looked up at him. The man was lost, completely lost.

They both were.

"We leave her here. Someone will find her and make sure she's looked after. We go home and forget it. We forget her." He knew it was wrong. He knew at that very moment his life had changed forever, and that in the words he'd just uttered was a death. Not Carol's and not Pat's but his own.

He dropped to one side and for a few minutes, the three of them lay in the grass with faces turned to the stars. They were starting to fade.

"We need to get home." Jack stood up and offered his hand to Pat who took it.

"What's that?" He could feel something in Pat's hand as he gripped it.

Pat opened his fist. In it was Carol's locket. It looked tiny and out of place in his grubby palm.

Jack took it and hurled it away. He hurled it back toward the lighthouse and it made a metallic 'clink' as it hit something. Anywhere would do, just not in the hand of his best friend, of his brother.

"Go!" He pushed Pat away, took a last look at Carol and started running. Tears flowed down his face for the first time since he'd asked his dad to tell him how his mum had died.

Chapter 18

"When he walked back through that door, I was mad. I was spitting feathers. He knew I was relying on him and he'd let me down. I was going to give him both barrels but when he looked at me, I knew something wasn't right. He wasn't hungover and he hadn't been fighting but something was wrong. He looked like he was lost. He had the same look in his eyes that you had the other morning when I showed you his note. Lost, simple as that. You look more than halfway there now too. But you ain't there yet. You will be though. You will be, lad."

*

"Where the hell have you been? You know…"

Joe took one look at his son and knew something was wrong, very wrong. He finished pulling his boots on and stood up.

"You in bother with the law?" he asked.

Jack stood in the doorway. Over his shoulder, Joe could see Pat in the car. He looked like he was a statue.

"What is it, son?"

If it was within his power, he could and would help him with anything. When the gearbox fell out of the Minx, he fixed it. When school told him Jack had been fighting, he fixed that. And when Pat's dad smashed the front room window and came looking for trouble, he fixed him. When Lizzy died, he took it on the chin and fixed himself.

"Will you come with me, Dad?" Jack looked over his shoulder at Pat who was sitting motionless in the front seat. "Will you come with us?"

"You need me?" he asked.

Jack nodded.

"Then I'll come."

Nobody spoke in the car on the way. Neither Jack nor Pat said anything to each other for half an hour but Joe's inner voice was deafening. It screamed at him to turn around and sit them both down to find out what was going on. But Jack had looked frightened, truly terrified, and that was all he could think about. His son needed him and whatever it was that was scaring him like that couldn't be fixed by sitting down at the table. There was a voice too. A voice that kept repeating itself, over and over again, 'Don't lose someone else you love.'

What stars were left were fading away quickly. In another hour, the sky would be the most beautiful azure and the sun would bounce like silver daggers off the surface of the sea. It would be a perfect day for setting lobster pots.

Jack pulled in and buried the car in the hedge. They were still a fair way from the lighthouse but the beacon was flashing clearly. He watched Jack shove Pat out of the passenger side and the three of them set off running toward the lighthouse. He had no idea what was coming but it wouldn't be good, that much was crystal clear.

They skidded down the bank and rounded the lighthouse perimeter wall. Part of Joe, a huge part of him, hoped that whatever it was he'd been brought here to see had vanished; had been blown away on the wind.

Jack pointed to a flock of seagulls which took off as they got closer. He heard Jack swear and behind him he could hear Pat sobbing.

"Oh God." Jack retched and Pat fell to the ground. There was a girl lying half-hidden in the meadow. The gulls had been at her. The gulls had been at her for some time and had stolen her eyes. There was nothing but two empty holes left.

"Tell me this isn't your doing, boys." Joe's mouth was dry and sour-tasting.

He looked at them in turn but neither of them would look back at him. Jack was bent double and Pat had buried his face in the grass.

He grabbed Jack and straightened him up. "Tell me you didn't do this." He looked into his son's eyes and saw the little boy he'd raised on his own. He cupped his face. "Tell me, Jack. Tell me this isn't your doing."

Tears rolled down his cheeks. "We think she took drugs, Pat came down here with…"

He closed his eyes and pushed Jack away. Pat was still on the ground face-down so Joe grabbed his hair and lifted his head.

"What have you done?" he yelled. Pat's eyes were closed. "Patrick Bailey, you tell me now or I'm going up to the

lighthouse and I'm bringing the police down here."

Pat lifted himself until he was sitting but he kept his eyes closed.

"She... I came down here with her and she had a fit or a seizure or something and she started being sick while I was... They'll lock me up, they'll lock Jack up too, Joe." Pat was almost wailing.

"We can say we found her, we can say we were just down here and found her..."

He heard Jack's voice but someone else was talking too. Someone in the hospital, a doctor, a small grey-haired doctor with bad breath was telling him something about Lizzy and about the baby. But he wasn't smiling like he should be. He wasn't congratulating him on being a father. No, he was saying something else. Something Joe didn't really understand. He didn't want to understand it. And then he was in another room and Lizzy was there and a nurse was holding Jack in her arms. Shouldn't my Lizzy be doing that? She should be holding Jack, not the nurse. We chose the name after her granddad. It's a good, strong name for a good strong baby.

But why were they covering Lizzy with a sheet? Why were they looking at him like that? Where's Jack gone now? Where are they taking him? No, no, no, he's my son. He's our little boy. You can't just take him away from me. Nobody will ever take him away from me. Never.

"The pair of you come here," Joe growled.

They both did as he ordered.

Pat touched his throat and opened his hand as if he expected to see something.

"The pendant," he whispered. "She had a silver pendant. It came off in my hand when we were…"

"Where is it?" Joe bellowed.

Jack pointed toward the lighthouse. "I threw it over there."

All three of them looked that way in silence for a moment until Joe shouted again,

"You take that poor girl and you carry her to the edge. You say a prayer for her and then you bury her in the ocean."

They both looked at him but they didn't argue. They didn't make a sound, they just lifted her gently and carried her to the edge. They looked at each other for a moment and then closed their eyes.

"I'm sorry," he heard Pat wail.

They dropped her into the waiting white foam of the ocean below. It was always hungry for new souls, forever had it been that way.

Nobody was taking his boy away from him again. Nobody.

"I'm sorry," Joe whispered and turned his back on them.

*

Chris stared at his granddad for what felt like an eternity. Their eyes were locked together like adversaries preparing for battle, like boxers squaring up before a fight. But Chris didn't want to fight with Joe. He didn't know what he wanted to do. He wasn't exactly sure how he felt about him at that moment in time.

"That's why they're here," Joe whispered.

Chris was momentarily confused. "Who?"

"Lizzy and Jack. They're here because *she* wants you, she

wants you and she wants Ollie." He leaned across the table. "They're upstairs. They're in his room."

Chris pushed his chair away from the table. "I need some air." He opened the door and walked around to the garden. He didn't know how to handle this, no idea at all. Whether or not Pat had contributed to Carol's death, there was no way of knowing. Whether or not they could have done anything to help her, again there was no way of knowing. Maybe she'd taken something other than pot, something that she had no business taking, there was no way of knowing that either. A lot of what happened was up for debate. But what was certain was that they had disposed of her body before anyone, any of her family, had been given the opportunity to say goodbye properly.

He clutched his head with both hands. God this was so… so fucking messy and confusing. What would he have done in Joe's shoes? It was easy to say he'd have gone to the police, but would he? Would he risk putting Ollie through an investigation when there was another way out? Would he risk losing his son and another boy he considered a son when he'd already lost his wife? He shook his head. What was the saying? Never judge a man until you've walked two moons in his moccasins.

He walked back to the house. One thing for absolute definite in all of this was that nobody and nothing was going to harm Ollie in any way. And he wasn't going to put all his trust in two ghosts either.

He walked back inside and found Joe making a cup of tea.

"I did see her down on the slipway, didn't I? She was there then, wasn't she?"

Joe put two mugs down. "Yes, she was. I think Jack was still trying to help her, even then."

"But she didn't look like she does now. She wasn't as…"

"Angry?"

"Yes, there wasn't this blackness around her, this awful stench of corruption coming out of her."

"Look, I don't have the answers, maybe over time these things grow darker and angrier. Maybe. I don't know, Christopher. I don't know!"

"Hello, boys!" Lou walked in, quickly followed by Ollie.

"Look what I've got!" He ran straight up to Chris and swiped him across the back of the head with the foam sword. "How d'you like that then?"

There were still a thousand things going round in Chris's head but he snapped out of it the instant Ollie came into the room. His life-force was infectious.

"I'll show you how I like it, shall I?" He turned around and made a grab for him, but Ollie was already off.

He looked up at Lou. "Good day?"

She bent down and kissed him. "Tiring."

She kissed Joe too. "Is the kettle still warm?"

Joe stood up. "I'll make you one. You look like you could do with a sit down."

Lou sat at the table and silently mouthed something to Chris. He didn't get all of it but he got the gist. He looked toward the front room to make sure Ollie wasn't in earshot. "It's okay, we've had a good talk. We're not going mad, Lou.

Granddad understands."

He watched Joe pour the boiling water into Lou's mug. He couldn't tell Lou about Carol, or about his dad and Pat's part in her death. Nor could he tell her about Joe's role in it. Maybe one day, long after Joe was gone, he'd do some research and try to find out who she was and find her family, but for now he had his own family to protect. That came first.

"Who is she?" It was the most natural and obvious question but he wasn't prepared for it. Neither of them was.

He had to say something before Joe did. Joe was in the mood for spilling his guts but it wasn't the right time.

"God knows, but it definitely is the woman who was with my dad."

"Well, what does she want?"

Joe put the mug of tea down in front of Lou. "She wants revenge."

That was it, it was simple. She wanted revenge for what his dad and Pat had done. Now neither of them was left, she wanted the next in the bloodline. She wanted him and she wanted Ollie.

"For what?" Lou looked at them both.

Joe opened his mouth but Chris jumped in. "That's what we've been trying to work out all day. Something Dad and Pat did when they were younger. This has been going on for years, Lou." He slid the folder over to her. "This is Pat's work."

She took it and looked inside. "Jesus." She flicked through it and pushed it back. "I don't want to look anymore. Did your dad have anything like this?"

He looked back to Joe. "I'd have to speak to Mum about that. But it's all making sense now. His moods, his depression, all of it was connected to what happened when…"

Lou waited for him to finish. "When? When what?"

"When they were lads. I don't know but now Pat's gone, she's coming for me and she's coming for Ollie."

Lou got up from the table and poured the tea away. From the front room, Chris could hear cartoons on the television.

"And your plan? You've been sitting here all day, so you've got to have a plan." She edged past Joe and took a few steps toward the front room.

Chris bit his lip. There was no plan. He didn't know what to do. He looked up at Joe who stared blankly back. If Joe didn't know what to do then they really were in trouble.

"You're safe here," he said.

"Safe?" Lou turned on him. "I don't feel safe anywhere, Joe. Not after what I saw in…"

"Lizzy will keep him safe." Joe spoke as if his dead wife were standing right beside him.

Lou shook her head and looked straight at Chris. "I'll tell you one thing right now. Nobody touches my boy." She turned back to Joe. "Not Lizzy and not that bitch, whoever she is." She stamped out of the room and went to Ollie.

Joe looked grey. His cheeks had lost the rosy glow they always had, and his body looked like nothing more than a clothes hanger. Most of all, he just looked tired.

"I need to have a lie down," he said and walked slowly away.

Joe was beaten. His years of fixing things for everyone and for himself were coming to an end. There was no point in looking to him for the answer because he didn't have one. Why had she never come for him, though? She'd haunted Pat for most of his life and probably his dad too but why not Joe? His part had been significant but he'd never touched the girl, he'd just told the boys to dispose of her. To bury her in the sea. Maybe that was it.

Chris rubbed his face. He was the only one who could do something now. He wouldn't have Ollie put through any more of this. The question was, what could he do?

Chapter 19

Chris hadn't gone off to sleep yet. He was surprised Lou had managed it. He usually slept naked, but something told him to keep his shorts on tonight and they kept riding up in uncomfortable places. There hadn't been any conversation since the discussion at the kitchen table. Not that the house had been silent, but any noise, any talk or questions, were directed toward Ollie. Joe came downstairs briefly to have a sandwich with them then went back upstairs quickly after that. He hadn't gone to The Queen's Head for his game of dominoes.

The house had changed. The air inside the house had changed. The air they expelled during their conversation was tainted and sour and it made everything smell old. It wasn't the same cottage he'd spent so much time growing up in. It wasn't the same cottage he'd been in last night or the night before. It had been altered and not for the better.

Lou muttered something in her sleep and twitched her

legs in a series of spasms. She was dreaming. About what, he could only guess but she moved as if she were fighting.

He went over and over the story in his head until his brain ached with it. It was awful, truly terrible what had happened and mistakes had been made by all of them. Joe, his dad and Pat had lost themselves that night. In doing so, they had forced him and Ollie down a deep, dark tunnel from which he couldn't think of a way to escape.

The house creaked, as it always did in the night. Sometimes it groaned too if the day had been particularly hot. The rafters and beams supporting the roof eased themselves into position for the night like an old man preparing to sleep. He rolled over and closed his eyes. Tomorrow was a new day and with the light might come some ideas about what he could do.

The stairs creaked and he opened his eyes. A moment passed without further sound and he allowed his eyes to close again.

They creaked again. Twice. Like something, or someone, was very slowly coming up the stairs. He held his breath and waited.

It happened again, and again it was very slow. Was the house still…

Then it was like a pianist running his fingers up the keys as the stairs rumbled together in an almighty crescendo.

Chris was out of bed before the sound had stopped and he threw open the bedroom door. In front of him stood the figure of a young woman. It was the young woman he'd seen down at the slipway with his dad. A young woman with a tangle of chestnut hair which fell over her shoulders.

"Carol," he whispered.

She turned toward him and her eyes were beautiful and dark. Her eyes were there again. She was whole but she was sad. Tears fell like crystals.

"I'm sorry," he whispered and took a step toward her. "My dad, Pat, Joe, they're all sorry." He was aware that Lou was standing behind him because he could feel her breath on his shoulder.

The door to Ollie's room creaked. "No," Chris whispered. "No, Ollie."

Then it banged open and Ollie was standing there in his astronaut pyjamas, rubbing his eyes. "Mummy?" he called out.

Carol smiled at Chris and one by one her teeth fell to the floor and those crystal tears turned to murky, festering water. Her eyes slid away, leaving only black holes and despair.

She turned to Ollie and lifted a finger. Her voice echoed throughout the house.

"I can see you."

Ollie fell back into his room. His body twitched twice on the carpet and a great torrent of water ran from his mouth like a river.

He's drowning, thought Chris. He's drowning just like I was, just like Dad did. But it's happening inside the house!

Lou pushed him out of the way, screaming "Leave him alone you fucking bitch! Leave him alone!" She ran to Ollie who was coughing up the slimy depths of the Atlantic Ocean onto the carpet.

Joe almost fell out of his room. "This is my house!" he shouted, but he was immediately thrown back against the door and crumpled to the floor.

"You can have me," Chris shouted. "Take me, I'll come with you but please leave my boy!" He watched Ollie's poor little body convulse and twitch in Lou's arms.

"Lizzy?" Joe's voice was weak but it came through the madness. "Lizzy!" he roared and this time there was no doubting the strength that still flowed through his veins.

The house creaked and groaned again and then Ollie's room slammed shut. The force of it made the house shake. It locked Lou and Ollie in there together.

Carol turned back to him and screamed. The sound it made was so deep and so low that Chris felt his eardrums vibrating in his head. He covered his ears but he could feel the thin membranes of his eardrums stretching to their limits.

And then she was gone.

Chris ran across the hall and pushed Ollie's door. It wouldn't give way. He put his shoulder to it but still it wouldn't open.

"Lou! Open the door."

He could hear her crying on the other side. "Lou!" He banged his fist on the door.

"Lizzy? She's gone." Joe was beside him and he put his hands on the door. "She's gone away, it's safe."

The door swung slowly open. Lou was on the floor kneeling beside Ollie who was trembling, but at least he was conscious. There was no sign of the water but his face was wet, wet from tears.

Chris dropped to his knees and held Ollie's head against his chest. Ollie was sobbing but he was alive. He was alive.

He looked at Lou. "The water. I thought he was drowning. I thought…"

"Water? There wasn't water, Chris. Just her eyes. Just those holes." She was crying too and he pulled her close.

"Daddy, make it stop. Make her stop it." Ollie's words broke his heart. With every sinew in his body he wished he could make this stop. Make *her* stop. But what could he…

He knew. In that instant, he knew what he must do. What he must do to make this stop. What he must do to protect his son. What his dad had wanted to do to protect him.

He kissed Ollie's head and smelled his hair. It was mango, his favourite shampoo.

He pulled away and held Ollie's face. "I'll make it stop, Ollie. I'll stop her."

He kissed his head again and turned to Lou.

"I need to do something, Lou. I need to do it for Ollie and for Dad, Pat and Granddad. And for me." He kissed her gently and smiled. "I love you."

Lou grabbed Ollie and held him to her again. "I love you too. Just help him, please."

He stood up and looked at Joe. The man looked angry, really angry. "Nobody comes in my house without my say-so. Nobody."

Chris squeezed past him and into the bedroom. He dressed quickly and walked back to the landing. Joe was still standing looking down at Lou and Ollie.

Chris patted him on the shoulder. "I'll see you in a while."

Joe didn't turn around or acknowledge that Chris had gone. It was probably better that way.

Chapter 20

Chris pulled into the car park. The tyres crunched over the loose stones as he drove straight to the bottom end; the end where the ambulance had been when they loaded Pat into it. He didn't remember a single inch of the drive down here, not a single bend along the mile-long stretch of lane.

He stopped the car and looked down over the cove. The last time he'd sat in a car here had been with his dad, eating ham and mustard sandwiches. The mustard stung his nose and made his eyes run but he hadn't let his dad see. His dad loved ham and mustard and because of that he would too. Whether he liked it or not.

It was all so simple really. Pat knew it and his dad had known. They knew where it had to end and yet Dad hadn't been given the time. He'd been too busy saving his son to give his life freely. To give her what she wanted.

But that was where it must end. It ends here and now with him. The line stops. He walks down that slipway into the sea and lets it take him where it may. He gives his life and Ollie keeps his sanity and his life. Simple.

His dad hadn't been weak. Quite the opposite. He'd written that note, knowing what he had to do to keep his son safe. It was all so very logical. Now he had to do the same thing.

He opened the car door and was immediately hit by the wind. It was what Joe referred to as a South-Westerly and was usually followed by rain, or a storm. The smell was the same though. That clean, fresh smell that came from the ocean. Nothing could capture it.

It was pitch black but if he closed his eyes, he could remember everything about the place, about that day. He lifted his eyes toward the headland where they had watched the waves and listened to the eternal rumble of sea against rock. In the distance, the lights from the houses at Sennen, and the building on Land's End farther along, twinkled like stars in the sky. There were no stars tonight though. The clouds had seen to that.

Would Ollie understand? Not at first he wouldn't. No boy could ever understand why their dad chose to leave him but in time he would. Like him, in time he'd see what had to be done. Chris took his mobile phone out of his pocket. There was no signal with which to send a message to Lou but that was good. He would just type out a message and leave it in the car. When they found it, the message would be there for Ollie, for them both.

He typed five words. *I'm sorry, I love you.* The screen glowed brightly in the gloom and the cursor blinked –

hungry for more words. But there were no more, not really. He put the phone in the holder on the dashboard and watched the glow fade then darken completely.

He started down the path. Past the fishermen's huts and lobster pots, with the strong scent of the day's catch, and stopped at the top of the slipway. What had he expected to find when he got here? Her? Pat, or his dad? It was empty. Nobody was waiting for him.

It was loud down here, much louder than he remembered. When he caught up with his dad on that day, he skidded and fell just here. He'd seen his dad pulling her out of the water, trying to save her, but she couldn't be saved. She was already dead. Had he seen that or had he seen what his own dad's conscious was seeing? All those years of guilt and all those years of regret had changed him into a man he should never have been. It had changed him and it had changed his son. Chris wouldn't allow that to happen again.

The first few drops of rain fell on his face. He sat down and tipped his head backwards. A few drops quickly became a downpour and within seconds his clothes were soaked through. His flesh prickled at the sensation. He could sit here for hours like this and listen to nature do what it did best. How long had Pat done the same? How long had Pat waited with a knife in his hand and contemplated what was coming next?

The sea was simmering. Soon it would boil and rage along with the wind and rain. He could hear it sliding up the slipway toward him, tempting him to take those first few steps. He edged forward and lay back. He wouldn't take those steps, he would allow the ocean to take him away instead.

It felt like an eternity had passed but he heard the wave break and for the first time felt it slip up his jeans and sting his flesh. Christ, it was cold. As cold as it had been on that day. It slid away but the next one rose higher, then the waves broke on his feet and tried to snatch him away. It would come soon. The wave in the series that was braver and fiercer than the others. The one that destroyed sandcastles and made families run up the beach clutching their blankets and flasks. It would come and drag him away. It was always looking for the opportunity to do just that. The ocean didn't care who it was.

As the water crept up his body, the shivers and aches started to force groans from him. But as the first draft of salt water entered his mouth, his voice was silenced. He closed his eyes. It was coming and Ollie would be safe.

The power of the wave shocked him and his first instinct was to fight against it. To grab onto the concrete with his fingernails and stop it dragging him under, to stop it dragging him away from his wife, from his son and from Joe. But he knew that wasn't how things were supposed to be. He was to give himself freely.

A second wave crashed against him and he knew he'd not been dragged but shoved sideways. It would be the same place as he had fallen all those years ago. He would hold onto life for as long as he could. He wouldn't take that breath that filled his lungs with water yet but he wouldn't fight its arrival. There was a symmetry here, wasn't there? An awful symmetry that seemed to be written somewhere in fate. And yet where was she to witness it? Where was she to witness what she had so long fought for? Where was she to say those words: *I can see you.*

His head collided with something but the pain paled beside the freezing ache in his bones. Where was she? Where was…?

He felt his body being dragged upwards and his shoulder almost popped from its socket. This was the end. He opened his mouth to take that final breath.

"Get out of there you stupid bastard!" His body was slung onto the concrete and he opened his eyes.

Joe was looking down at him.

"Granddad?"

"You stupid bugger. What the bloody hell do you think you're doing?" He felt a kick in his ribs. "You're not going to leave that little boy without a daddy. I won't allow it." He kicked him again. From somewhere, Joe had summoned enough strength to drag him out and was now beating him up.

"Look at you! Just bloody look at you!" Joe kicked him again but this time there was hardly any strength in it.

Chris lay stunned. He'd been plucked out of the ocean for the second time in his life but it looked like Joe might kill him anyway.

"But it's the only way… I don't know what to do."

Joe grabbed his t-shirt and wrenched him upright. "Well neither do I but I know this isn't it. I ought to thrash the living daylights out of you and I still might." He shoved him up the slipway.

"Where are we going?" he asked.

"Pendeen. You're going to Pendeen."

Chapter 21

Joe berated him all the way back from Hawk's Cove. He slapped him around the back of the head a couple of times to emphasise his point too. Chris had never seen Joe lose his temper before but he well and truly blew his top this time. He couldn't remember hearing him swear either but every other word was a profanity.

Had it been such a stupid idea? There seemed to be this underlying symmetry about it all. Pat never had kids – through never finding a partner or through choice, Chris couldn't say – but maybe he knew what having a child would do to him. He'd witnessed it first hand in his dad though, that was for sure.

Chris pulled the car up outside Joe's cottage. His head was aching, in fact his entire body was throbbing, from the sea and the beating from Joe.

"Why has she never come for you? Why me, why Ollie? We're not to blame for this. Dad, Pat and you were. Not us." Now Chris was warming up, he was getting angry too.

"It wasn't the sea burial we gave her," said Joe. "It was something that happened whilst only they were there. Something they did. What I did will be judged later but what they did, that's what she's mad about. You need to go up there and make amends." Joe grabbed the back of his neck. "And that doesn't mean throwing yourself in the drink. Got that?"

Chris tried to nod but Joe's grip was strong. "And you'll look after Ollie and Lou?"

"And so will my Lizzy."

"They don't need to know about what just happened, do they?"

Joe released his hold and opened the door. "Not from me they don't."

He slammed the door and walked inside. The lights in the kitchen were on and as Chris drove away, there was a fleeting glimpse of Ollie at the window. He slammed his palm into his forehead.

"Stupid, stupid bastard." Nobody was touching his son.

*

The lighthouse beacon was visible long before he turned off the main road. It winked at him every four seconds to show him the way. He had no idea what he was going to do once he got there, what he was supposed to do. But Joe was right, this was where he had to be.

He looked at the light as it swung over the ocean. "I can see you," he whispered. And in the back of his mind, an answer was given. *And I can see you.*

He stopped on the grassy bank and left the engine running. The car's lights lit up a sheet of heavy rain as it fell on the coast. It seemed to be raining sideways as the wind whipped it through the headlights. Joe was right about the weather, he always was, and the storm was upon them. Upon them all.

He touched the door handle and paused. His phone was still in the dashboard holder and as soon as he swiped his finger across the screen, his last unsent message was still there. The cursor blinked as he deleted the five words. He stuffed it in his pocket and climbed out. Nobody need know about what he tried to do.

The wind took the door from his grip and slammed it for him. It had been strong down at Hawk's but it was nothing in comparison to this. His clothes were already wet, the wind drove them onto his body and stuck them in place like glue.

"What do you want?" he yelled. "Come on, what do you want?"

He stood at the top of the bank and put his hand on the lighthouse perimeter wall. There was nothing, just the scream of the wind and the roar of the ocean. He had to go down. He had to go and find the place Joe had described, whether or not his head and stomach told him that it was a bad idea. They hadn't said that when he was lying on the slipway at Hawk's Cove an hour ago though, so if he couldn't trust them, what was left? Instinct. That was all that was left. Blind instinct.

He gripped the wall and took a few steps down the bank

before he slipped and rolled the rest of the way. The sound of the ocean grew closer and closer until he managed to sink his hands into the dirt to hold himself steady. His injured hand screamed in agony and he let the pain come out of his mouth in a great torrent of expletives. The words were carried away in an instant.

He got to his feet. Rain was dripping from his nose and running into his mouth, and he could taste blood. The rusted fence posts were still there; if nobody had fixed them by now, they never would. He stepped closer and looked over the edge. It made his stomach lurch at the sight of the spitting waves below.

He followed the wall round until he was in the meadow. Joe, Pat and his dad had all stood in this place and decided what they were going to do with Carol. The thought of it was enough to make him angry.

"You took the drugs! It wasn't their fault!" His voice was nothing to the forces of nature that were happening around him.

He ran across the meadow, with no idea where he was going or what he would find. "They were sorry, and they've paid for what they did. Please, please Carol."

He tripped and fell to the ground "And I'm sorry, for what they did." He banged his hands into the earth sending another ripple of pain through his arm. "I'm sorry!"

At that moment, it was as the world had been told to *shh*. The waves stopped roaring and the wind stopped screaming and all that was left were four words.

"I can see you."

It was as clear as anything he'd ever heard. It shook him to the core, as it had done each and every time the words had been uttered. He fumbled in his pocket and found his phone. It had a torch on it and he pressed the button to switch it on.

"I can see you," she said again.

He slipped and slid and scrambled around the meadow. Her voice was everywhere. It was in the wind, in the sea, in the grass and in his head. He shone the torch into the darkness but it was pathetic.

She was everywhere.

"I can see you."

He stopped moving. The voice had come from behind. A chill ran through his body and made him shiver.

"I can see you," she repeated.

His hands were shaking but he held the phone like a shield and turned around slowly. He didn't want to move but someone had switched the automatic button inside his head. The torch lit up a face, as pretty as any he'd ever seen. She was beautiful and her deep, dark eyes were like, like… Had someone followed him here?

He opened his mouth to say something but as he did, her face started slipping away. Slowly at first as if she were melting, then faster and faster until all that was left were two voids, two deep voids and he was falling into them.

"I can see you." She spat the words through teeth that fell from her mouth as she spoke and festering, murky water dripped from her lips.

He wanted to close his eyes. He wanted to do it so badly

but he knew that if he did, she would follow him in there. She would always be there. She would always be inside him, just as she had always been inside his dad and Pat. She would always be inside Ollie too now, unless he could do something. Anything…

"I can see you, I can see you, I can see you…" she repeated over and over again until he thought his mind would simply curl up in a little ball and send him to the cliff…

The foghorn boomed into the night and jolted him. It sent him reeling backwards away from her, crashing into the perimeter wall. He cried out as the back of his head smashed into the wall. The pain was excruciating but the force of it knocked her out of his head, momentarily.

He held the torch up again but he had no need, she was almost on him.

The foghorn blasted again and the depth of its tone shook the earth beneath his body. It had sounded before on the night he was here with Pat. There was no fog then. She was almost on him again and wherever he ran, wherever he took Ollie, she would always be there.

The wind whipped across his face, snapping it out to sea. The lighthouse shot a beam of light across the water. There was no fog. There was a storm, there couldn't be any fog.

It blasted again in agreement and the creature Carol had become looked up at the great funnel. Briefly and just for a split-second, Chris saw something other than the blackness; he saw a star, or something that shone. But then it was gone.

"I can see you!"

He turned before he was trapped by her eyes and jumped up. He reached the top of the wall and clung on with his fingers. The hand that had beaten Tallack was broken in places that could never be fixed but he poured his strength into it and hauled himself upwards onto the top of the wall. He looked back briefly, watched her rise as if there was no wind. Hair as black as the deepest-dwelling seaweed blew out from her head.

He was transfixed again. "No," he muttered and fell backwards off the wall. The rattle his bones made as he landed was overshadowed by the bellow of the foghorn, but he kept hold of his phone and pointed it into the darkness.

The pendant.

The pendant had bounced off something metallic when his dad had thrown it. He'd taken it from Pat's hand and thrown it away like a piece of junk.

As he rolled over, he could feel the tendrils of her breath on his neck as she whispered into his ear.

"I... can... see... Ollie."

He screamed and flailed his arms at her but it was like punching fresh air. His blows did nothing. She smiled down on him with those rotten teeth and oh so dark eyes. So dark, so full of grief and anger and...

The foghorn boomed but it sounded softer now, like it was losing strength.

"Your pendant." His voice was little more than a whisper but it pushed her away and suddenly she was a woman. She was Carol again.

He jumped up and sprinted to the foghorn. It was in

there. It had to be. As he reached it, he could feel her behind him again but he wouldn't look at her. No matter the guilt he felt, the fear or the anger. He would not look at her again.

He grabbed the rim of the horn and looked inside. It was as wide as the span of his arms and as deep.

"It's in there!" he shouted, as much through hope as expectation, his voice landing with a dull thud.

He reached inside.

"Ollie," she whispered. She was retreating away from him. She was going back to the house to get Ollie.

"No, no, no!" He shone the little light into the horn and a glimmer rebounded. His heartbeat went up another notch, if that were possible, as he reached inside and touched it. It was just within his reach but his fingers were so cold he could barely close them around it. He stretched every sinew in his body, pushed his fingers down and dragged it out.

He withdrew his hand and turned around "I have it!" he roared, but she was gone. There was nothing but the night around him now.

"No more." He dropped to his knees. "No more, Carol." He held the pendant up to the sky. It was as light as a feather and in places had perished to nothing. Whatever chain it had been attached to was still at the bottom of the foghorn but he hoped this was enough. The top half of the locket was missing and there was nothing inside, nothing he could see at least.

There was a silence again, as nature took a deep breath, and then she was there, staring at him with those bottomless pits. He held the pendant higher. "Take it," he whispered.

She lowered her head and slowly she became the girl again. She became Carol.

"Take it," his voice trembled.

But she didn't reach for it. She just touched her neck where it should have been. Where it had probably been on the night she died.

"Take it, please!"

"I can see you!" She spoke softly, without menace or threat. Her eyes were only on the locket.

"I can see you, Mum." As she spoke, a shiny locket appeared at her neck. She touched it, twirled it between her fingers. "I can see you, Mum."

And then the locket blew away like dust and Carol simply floated away into the darkness.

Chris fell back, stared at the dark sky above his head and allowed the tears to flow down his cheeks. The wind tried to whip them away and the rain tried to dilute them. But they slid down his cheeks, tasting like the saltwater had done when his dad rescued him.

Chapter 22

Chris stood on the headland and watched Ollie skimming stones across the sea. The sun bounced off the ocean in a silvery haze. It was beautiful.

Ollie looked up at him and gave him a thumbs-up sign. He returned it with two thumbs.

Six months had passed since the night at Pendeen. They had been long months. Long months filled with nightmares, long sleepless nights spent sharing the bed with a seven year old boy and a wife.

This was the place, the exact spot where he'd stood with his dad on that day. That was a huge step forward for him. He'd watched the waves come in as the storm approached. The sounds were the same, the waves, the wind and the birds. It was all here and it would always be here. Hawk's Cove had been here long before it had ever been called Hawk's Cove.

He looked up at the car park. Joe was up there in the car.

His legs had started giving way and his daily walks to the pub were a thing of the past. They were weekly visits now, usually on curry night with his grandson and great-grandson.

"Make mine as pokey as Lollipop's," Ollie had said to Susie. When the curry came out and Ollie had taken a mouthful, his face turned a very bright red.

"Good isn't it, lad?" Joe had laughed and Ollie hadn't been very well the next day, but he never wanted to miss curry night at The Queen's Head. He just asked for less poke.

They had moved here permanently two months ago, although in the intervening time, Joe had never been alone for more than a few weeks. One, both or all of them had stayed at some point. Now the move was permanent, he seemed happier than ever. He looked tired and sometimes Chris heard him talking to people who weren't there. Or rather, people who weren't visible to him. He never did it when Ollie was around though.

Lou hadn't asked questions about what happened. She would in time, and when he told her, that would be when they'd go looking for Carol's family. Lou wouldn't allow it to be any other way.

But Carol hadn't come back. She had what she needed.

Atonement. That was what Carol had wanted and the only person capable of giving it to her was him. His father had thrown her pendant away like it was worthless trash. It might not have been the most expensive piece of jewellery but it meant everything to her. How could she ever be at peace without the thing she treasured above all else?

Chris froze. Ollie was on the slipway and standing beside him were two people. People he didn't recognise. Where was Lou?

"Lou!" he shouted but they were too far away. She must have been sitting at the top of the slipway.

Who were they? Both of them put a hand on Ollie's shoulders and it sent a cold chill down his back. He sprinted along the path and skidded at the turn for the cove. The smell of lobster pots was fleeting but it still held a memory, not a good one either.

He reached the slipway and almost fell into Lou. She was sitting reading a book.

"Watch it!" She edged away from him.

He looked down the slipway at Ollie. "Who were they?"

"What?" She shielded her eyes from the sun. "Who?"

He pointed at Ollie. "The couple who were standing there!"

Lou looked down at Ollie. "There's nobody else here. Just us." She touched his ankle. "He's safe, don't worry."

He looked down and tried to smile. "I thought I saw…" He stopped. He was just over-sensitive about Ollie, that was all.

"I'll go and throw a few stones with him for half an hour."

He walked down to Ollie. The tide was out and the bottom of the slipway was covered in a tangle of seaweed.

"How's it going, big man?"

Ollie threw another stone into the calm sea. It skimmed

three times and then sank. "See that?"

Chris stepped off the side and gathered a handful of flat pebbles. "Not bad, watch this." He threw the stone. It skipped across the surface twice and then sank.

"That's rubbish, Dad."

"It was just the wrong stone, that's all." He pushed through the stones and found another.

"So, who were those two?"

Ollie wound his arm back. "Don't know, just a couple of people." He threw the stone and crouched down for another.

"What did they say to you?" Chris asked.

"Something about taking care of me." He stopped searching for stones and looked up. "One was called Lizzy and the other was called Jack."

The End

Printed in Great Britain
by Amazon